CHAPTER ONE

Olivia didn't tell the audience it was her final show. It was a small crowd that wasn't here to see her and they wouldn't care. She'd simply try to give her best performance ever, put all of her passion into these final six songs, and then leave the stage to focus on other areas of her life.

There was a time when she couldn't imagine giving up on her dream. That time was before ten years of performing in tiny, often crappy, sticky-floored venues for little or no money and less than adoring crowds. Not *hostile* crowds—she'd managed to make it a decade without anybody flinging a beer bottle at her head—but frequently lethargic ones. She helped pass the time until the headliner showed up.

Olivia loved music more than anything. She was also finally starting to accept that she might not be very good at it.

She wasn't a talentless hack. People didn't flee the venue with their hands over their ears. But they also didn't rush over to her merch table to buy stickers or CDs. People occasionally told her that they'd enjoyed her set, yet she hadn't really accumulated much of a fan base. It was rare that anybody showed up specifically because of her. She certainly didn't have any groupies, and she even would have been happy with a creepy, stalkerish one.

The realization that she might be average at best came after she, against her better judgment, took a day job that she suspected she might not hate. And she'd been correct. It was a decent-paying, satisfying job with friendly co-workers—the worst possible thing for her artistic soul. She still wanted to be a successful musician, but she was no longer *hungry* for it. Though Olivia craved the adoration of an audience, she also really liked medical and dental benefits.

She'd toyed with the decision of quitting music for a while. What clinched it was when she decided not to tell any of her co-workers about tonight's performance, because she was worried that they might have to tell a little white lie when they praised her.

So this was it.

The manager gave her the signal, and she walked up on stage with her acoustic guitar and played her heart out.

She'd thought she might cry when her set was over, which would be awkward for the audience since they didn't know this was the end of an era, but she felt strangely calm when it was over, as if it wasn't real. She felt almost happy. Relieved.

Olivia walked off stage to a smattering of applause. She got a beer and leaned against the back wall, collecting her thoughts.

A man walked over to her. He looked a few years older than her, maybe mid-thirties. He wore tinted glasses

MY PRETTIES

JEFF STRAND

and had one of those gigantic hipster beards. He had a small bandage on his neck. "Great set," he said.

"Thank you."

He switched his own bottle of beer from his right hand to his left before reaching out to her. "Greg."

She shook his hand. "Olivia."

"Really impressive stuff up there."

"Thanks. Hey, I'm not trying to be bitchy, but I need to decompress a little, and I'm not looking to get hit on right now."

Greg held up his left hand and tapped his wedding ring. "Not my intention."

"And being married would stop you?"

"I swear I'm not trying to bang you. All I want is sixty seconds of your time. Who's your manager?"

"I don't have one."

"Really?"

"Really."

"Then I'm glad I came over to talk to you. I'm not sure where you're looking to go with your career, but I'll bet you have higher aspirations than playing at this place."

Olivia shrugged. Though Greg seemed nice enough, he was one performance too late.

He reached into his back pocket, took out his wallet, and withdrew a business card. It said *Gregory Coffer – Artist Representation* with a phone number and website. There were a couple of musical notes in the upper right corner. He tucked his wallet back into his pocket while Olivia stared at the card.

"You handle musicians?" she asked.

"Yep."

She handed the card back to him. "Thanks. I've been

through this before. No offense, but I've had managers promise me the world."

"I'm not promising you the world. I'm not saying I can get you into Madison Square Garden. I'm saying that I can get you way better gigs than this one. You write all of your own songs, right?"

Olivia nodded.

"I can tell. There's a certain energy when a performer does her own material, songs that she created, that she's passionate about. You've got too much talent to be playing to a dozen people who are too busy checking their phones to experience what you have to offer. You should be opening for bigger acts at better venues. And then other people should be opening for you. It'll be done in baby steps, and it'll be a lot of hard work, but you've got something special. I can help you."

Olivia laughed. She couldn't help herself.

Greg raised an eyebrow. "I don't get the joke."

"I quit," she said. "Tonight was my farewell performance. I'm done with this business."

"Oh. Well, that breaks my heart. I'm honored that I could be here for it. Wish I'd met you sooner. I feel like I could've changed things."

"Maybe."

"Can I at least buy a signed CD from you?"

"I didn't set up a merch table this time."

"Well, shit. I spend every night going around trying to find undiscovered talent like yours, and I got here too damn late. If I'm lucky, in a year or so I'll see you playing somewhere and find out that you changed your mind." He extended his hand. "Good luck to you, Olivia."

She sighed. Then she took a long swig of her beer, finishing off the bottle. "I need another drink," she said.

"How about you buy me one and we'll talk?"

"That would make me very happy."

"I'll almost definitely say no. But I'll listen to what you have to say."

"Fantastic." He pointed to the bottle. "Same kind?"

"Yes."

"Be right back."

Olivia watched Greg carefully as he walked over to the bar. He seemed like a genuinely nice guy, but that didn't mean he wouldn't try to slip something into her drink.

She couldn't believe this was happening. She'd spent long sleepless nights thinking about this decision. She'd cried in the bathroom at work over it. And now that she'd made peace with it, now that she felt *better* about her life, Greg was here to possibly make an offer that might cause her to forever wonder what might have been if she turned it down.

But she should turn it down. She should absolutely, positively, without question turn it down. Why go through all of the frustration again?

The bartender popped the bottles open and Greg brought them back to their table. He set hers in front of her, then held his up. "Cheers."

"Cheers." They clinked their bottles together.

"So let me be very blunt," said Greg. "If you've been struggling, it's not due to lack of musical talent, it's due to lack of stage presence."

Olivia grinned. "Are you saying I'm boring?"

"Not at all. You just put all of your focus on the songs and none on the talk. There should be anecdotes that go with each song. Jokes. Stuff to make the audience feel like they're your friend."

"I tried that. I was terrible at it."

"I can work with you. I swear, Olivia, I can take you to the next level. I'm not saying I can take you up here," he said, holding his hand high into the air, "but I promise I can take you here." He held up his hand at chest-level.

"Starting from where?"

Greg lowered his hand an inch. Then he chuckled. "Sorry, I don't want to undersell myself, but I don't want to move my hand too low and insult you. That was a no-win hand movement for me. All I'm saying is that I can help."

"I don't know."

"I like hearing that doubt in your voice. We're getting somewhere."

A woman, visibly drunk, stumbled into the booth, almost knocking over their beers. She looked directly at Olivia with unfocused eyes. "That. Was. Awesome."

"I beg your pardon?"

The woman pointed to the empty stage. "That. When you were up there. Those fuckin' songs. Didn't you see me grooving on you?"

"The way the lights are it's hard to see the people in the crowd, but I appreciate that. Thank you."

"No, thank *you*. Anyway, I wasn't trying to interrupt your date. Bye." The woman staggered away.

"Looks like I'm not the only one with fine musical taste," said Greg.

"That was weird. This doesn't happen to me. If it did, I never would've quit." Granted, the woman would probably be passed out in the restroom three minutes from now, but Olivia didn't mind if praise came from people too drunk to know what they were saying.

"I've never seen you before, but maybe thinking this was your last performance let you relax on stage."

"I wasn't relaxed."

"More relaxed than usual, though?"

"Nope. More stressed out. But I did try to go out with a bang. I don't know, what if I've been holding back all this time?"

Greg took a drink of his beer. "It's possible."

"Or it could be pure coincidence," Olivia said. "Fate trying to mess with me. The world putting a bunch of 'What if's?' into my brain just when I thought I figured everything out."

"But what's the risk? I'm not asking for any money. I work on commission. I'm asking for a little bit of your time. Time to let me fine-tune your performance, and time to play the better gigs I'm going to set up for you. I'm asking for a month. One month. One month for you to say, 'Oh, my career is going slightly better than it was a month ago.' No contract. Walk away whenever you want."

Olivia started to tell him no. She took a long drink of beer instead. "I'll have to think about it."

"That is totally fair. I'm not here to pressure you. All I ask is that you not throw away my card. You might go home and decide that you're not the least bit interested, and that's fine, but in a year, two years, if you have second thoughts, give me a call. I'm not lying when I say that I almost never see talent like yours. I wouldn't just say that. I mean, hell, it cost me an overpriced beer."

Olivia laughed and took another drink. "This has been a very strange night."

She finished the beer and started to lose track of their conversation. Greg offered to walk her out to her car, and she thought that it might be a good idea since he was very nice, so she let him guide her out of the club, and she couldn't remember if she'd already put her guitar back into her car, but she supposed it didn't matter because she doubted she'd ever play it again, though she should sell it instead of just leaving it there, but she might have put it in her car, there was no way to know for sure, and Greg wasn't really walking her in the direction of her car, which seemed bad at first but less bad when she decided that she shouldn't be driving anyway, because that would be reckless and irresponsible, and Greg was very nice to be taking care of her like this, and she felt bad that she didn't want to play music again, and he was so nice that he fastened her seat belt for her, just like she was his daughter, Olivia wished she had a daughter, just one, no need to get carried away, oh that was funny but she couldn't make her mouth laugh, she wanted to close her eyes and sleep forever but that would be rude but it was too late she'd already closed her eyes and she couldn't open them and she didn't want to open them and Greg sure was nice to her.

Olivia opened her eyes.

She was swaying back and forth.

Not from being drugged. She was in a cage suspended several feet above a cement floor, with her legs dangling free. There was almost no room to move—at her heaviest weight a few years ago, she probably wouldn't have fit in here. The top of the cage pressed against the top of her head. Her shoulders touched the sides.

She could turn her head. When she did, she saw that the windowless room contained a dozen cages, four rows of three, hanging by thick chains from the ceiling. More than half of the cages were occupied.

A wooden chair and a stepladder were in the far corner, next to a door.

The woman in the cage next to her was pale. Emaciated. Her eyes were open and she was looking at Olivia, but it was unclear if she was actually seeing her.

The other women—and they were all women— appeared to be dead. Three of them were dead without question. The other two *might* have been unconscious, but probably weren't. All of them were nightmarishly thin. Almost skeletal. One was literally skeletal.

The smell of rot was so overpowering that she had a coughing fit that lasted for almost a minute.

When she stopped coughing, Olivia screamed and screamed.

Then she forced herself to shut the hell up and take stock of the situation. Greg wasn't in the room. She could escape. Her mind was still fuzzy, but there had to be way out of this. One that all of those other doomed women had overlooked.

"Don't," said the woman in the cage next to her. Her voice was a weak rasp.

"Don't what?"

The woman blinked twice, hard, as if to focus. "Scream. It hurts my ears."

"Where are we?"

"Does it matter? Wait it out. It's not as bad once you stop feeling anything."

Olivia began to swing her feet. The cage rocked along with her.

"We've tried that. Tried all of that. Tried everything."

"Well, I'm not going to just sit here."

"Yes, you will. That's all you'll do. Sit here. He'll give you water. But no food. Never any food. Soon we'll be like the others."

"They all starved to death?"

"I think he got mad at the first one. That's what I heard. I wasn't here yet. The rest starved."

"We can escape," Olivia insisted. "If we work together, we can get out of this. There has to be a way."

The woman smiled. "You're cute."

"I'm not giving up."

"You will."

"When will he be back?"

"It doesn't matter."

"When?"

"Nobody knows."

Olivia's cage swung back and forth, missing the woman's by inches. They'd probably been specifically spaced out so that they wouldn't collide. And she couldn't imagine that the setup would be so flimsy that she could yank the cage out of the ceiling by swinging it, but she had to try *something*. She couldn't just sit here and die.

The cage did not pop free from the ceiling.

After a while she quit swinging.

Then she went back to screaming.

Of course the room was soundproofed. The other women would've thought to shout for help. She was wasting energy.

Her legs were dangling free. When Greg returned, she could lure him close to her, then kick him in the face. Break his nose.

That wouldn't do any good, though. She'd still be trapped in the cage.

She could talk to him. Reason with him. Convince him that she'd never tell anybody, not a soul. She didn't know what the other women had said to him. Maybe she could say something different. Something that would change his mind.

She screamed some more.

"You're hurting my ears," said the other woman, when Olivia finally stopped.

"There has to be a way out of this."

"You'll stop believing that. When he comes back, he'll sit in a chair and watch us. Just watch us. Quietly watch us starve."

CHAPTER TWO

*A*w, *shit,* thought Charlene as she walked into the back room and saw the new girl leaning against the wall, crying. Was she going to have to ask what was wrong? Try to console her? Should she just quietly step out of the room and hope she hadn't been seen?

The new girl immediately noticed the intrusion and quickly dabbed at her eyes. "Sorry. I'm sorry."

Charlene was pretty sure the new girl had said her name was Gertie. When introducing herself she'd said, "Yes, like Drew Barrymore in *E.T.*," so if Drew played somebody named Gertie in that movie, that was the new girl's name. Charlene had never seen *E.T.* and would not have thought to make that reference. An incredibly inappropriate alien comment *had* popped into her mind, but Charlene a) was at work, and b) had just met Gertie, so she'd used her filter and left the hilariously gross alien comment unsaid.

She was proud of this. Many things made it past her filter on any given day. Many, many things.

Gertie was attractive, though not Charlene's type. She

doubted Gertie had even a single tattoo. Charlene liked to be the corrupted and not the corrupter (though by now, at age twenty-six, it was difficult to find scenarios where she could say, "Goodness gracious, I've never done *that* before!"). Gertie looked wholesome. Not virginal, but not somebody who would let lovers choke her. Average height but extremely thin—not in an anorexic way, but still skinny as shit. She was probably fresh out of college and her tears were from the realization that her four-year degree had earned her a job as a server at a mediocre Italian restaurant.

"Everything okay?" Charlene asked. "I mean, obviously not, dumb question. What I mean is, is there anything I can do?"

"No. I just needed a minute to myself and somebody was already in the restroom."

"You sure?" Charlene didn't know why she'd asked if Gertie was sure. She'd been given a free pass to politely leave—why hadn't she taken it?

Gertie nodded. "A customer was horrible to me. It's no big deal. I'll get used to it."

"Which table?"

"Eight."

"The lady in the blue dress?"

"Yeah."

"She looks like a mega-bitch. Does she know you're new? You would've been shadowing Jason for your first couple of days, right?" Charlene had been off Tuesday and Wednesday. She'd spent all day Tuesday in her pajamas binge-watching television shows, and all day Wednesday helping her parents paint their house.

"Yeah. It wasn't even something I messed up. She's just one of those people who gets off on being mean to people who can't do anything about it. But again, it's no big deal. I've been kind of discombobulated lately and I wasn't ready for that right after I started my shift. It's literally the first table I've done on my own."

"Want me to take care of it?" Charlene asked.

"No, that's fine. You have your own tables."

"That's not what I meant."

"What did you mean?"

"Vengeance."

Gertie gave her a *"Surely you're kidding"* look, then quickly seemed to realize that Charlene was serious.

"Oh, no, no, no, that's not necessary at all. She wasn't that bad."

"She made you cry."

"Right. Yes, she was that bad. She's hellspawn. But, no, you don't need to do anything."

Charlene walked over to her. "I'll be completely honest with you. This job sucks and I don't care if I get fired or not. So I'm more than happy to make your problem go away."

"I don't want you to get in trouble."

"I just said that I don't care if I get fired. I'm not going to stab her in the eye with a fork. This will make you feel better, I promise."

"No. Don't do it."

"Sorry. The train is already in motion. If you want to stop me, you'll have to tackle me."

Charlene turned and left the back room. She walked over to the chef's station and picked up a tray that was meant for table fourteen, then strode into the dining area. She went over to table eight, where a middle-aged woman who looked like she clubbed dolphins for amusement sat across from a much older man who looked like he purchased the dolphins for her to club for amusement.

"Your server had a family emergency and had to leave," Charlene informed them.

The woman looked annoyed by this. The man shrugged and made a non-committal grunt.

"Who had the lasagna?"

"That's not our order," said the woman. To be fair, it legitimately wasn't her order, but the snotty-ass way she said this made it clear that Gertie was not exaggerating about her unpleasant nature.

"It's not?" Charlene asked. "Are you sure?"

"We're not senile. We remember what we ordered."

Charlene glanced back at the kitchen. Gertie stood in the doorway, watching closely, looking very nervous about what Charlene might do. She even looked like she might regret not tackling her. Oh well.

"Hmm. I was told to bring this plate of lasagna to you. Maybe I misheard. I can be so scatterbrained sometimes. They're forever telling me to get my head screwed on straight, but do I listen? Nope. Head's still on crooked. See?"

She tilted her head. Then she spilled the plate of lasagna all over the front of the woman's dress.

"Oh no!" said Charlene, as everybody in the restaurant turned to look. "Oh dear!"

"Goddamn it!" The woman stood up. Tomato sauce, cheese, and pasta slid down her dress.

"I'm so very sorry! I'm such a butterfingers!"

Charlene looked back at Gertie. She was staring in shock with her hand over her mouth. Charlene couldn't tell if she was pleased or not. It didn't matter—Charlene was pleased.

She set down the tray, then picked up a cloth napkin and dabbed at the woman's dress. "At least it wasn't spaghetti. That's way slimier. Let me help you."

The woman swatted her hand away. "Don't bother."

"My apologies. We won't charge you for the lasagna."

"I didn't order the goddamn lasagna!"

"It makes God sad when you use language like that."

The woman gave her a look of pure, raw hatred.

Charlene now had an extremely important decision to make. There was a large glass of Coke still on the tray. Would that be taking this too far? Or would that be taking this the exact right amount? Maybe the woman would appreciate having the warm pasta offset by an ice-cold soft drink. It might give her perky nipples. Everybody enjoyed perky nipples.

She picked up the tray, not yet having committed to a plan of action. The Coke might remain upright. It might not. It all depended on whether or not the woman stopped scowling in the next couple of seconds.

The woman did not stop scowling.

Charlene, wacky klutz that she was, not-accidentally tilted the tray, causing the Coke to topple over and splash all over the woman. Because the woman was standing, the soda hit lower than the lasagna had; otherwise it might've helped rinse off some of the tomato sauce. The woman let out a magnificent yelp.

"I can't believe I did that. It's like I forgot all of my balance training. I am so, so, so, so, so, so, so, so very sorry, ma'am."

"You stupid idiot!"

"Stupid idiot? I understand that you're upset, but there's no reason to be redundant."

"I want to speak to a manager."

"He'll be here soon. I'm sure he heard you yelp."

Charlene sat in the back room. Travis, the manager of Davey's Italian Grill who had nary a trace of Italian blood, sat across from her, looking stern. He rubbed his eyes, ran a hand through his graying hair, scratched the top of his head, rubbed his eyes again, sighed, and then spoke. "You know what I'm gonna say, right?"

"I'm fired?"

"Of course you're not fired. We're shorthanded enough as it is. I'm not gonna cut off my nose to spite my face."

"I never understood what that meant."

Travis looked surprised. "It means that if you're pissed off at your face, you don't cut off your nose, because it hurts."

"Wait, I did know what that one meant. I'm thinking of having your cake and eating it too."

"If you eat your cake, you no longer have it. You either have a piece of cake or you eat a piece of cake, but you can't do both."

"Got it," said Charlene. "If you weren't going to say that I'm fired, what were you going to say?"

"I'm docking your pay for the cost of her dry-cleaning bill."

"Oh."

"Do you agree that it's a fair consequence?"

"I never get my clothes dry-cleaned," said Charlene. "I don't know how much it costs."

"It's not that much."

"Okay, good."

"She says you did it on purpose."

"That doesn't sound like me."

"You're being sarcastic but it really doesn't sound like you," said Travis. "That's why I'm pretending to give you the benefit of the doubt."

"I appreciate that."

"She's been in here before. She's a nightmare. That doesn't mean you get to dump food on her. What if you'd injured her?"

"With lasagna?"

"What if she was allergic to tomatoes?"

"I didn't get any on her bare skin."

"But you could have. You didn't spill it on her knowing the exact trajectory the sauce would take. You spill lasagna on somebody with a tomato allergy and we've got serious legal problems."

"That did not occur to me."

"You're acting like this is a tongue-in-cheek conversation but I'm serious about the risk."

"I usually can't identify the tone of our conversations."

"This one is Angry Boss to Irresponsible Employee, but with affection."

"Noted. It'll never happen again. I was just mad because she made the new girl cry."

"I assigned Gertie her table on purpose. If you can survive that hag, you can handle any other customer. It was a test."

"She would've passed. She just needed a minute to compose herself. Gertie didn't give me permission to dump the lasagna on her. She tried to stop me, but only with words, so it didn't work."

"You don't need to protect her. She's not getting fired,

either. Pull another stunt like that, no matter how funny and satisfying, and this will be a very different conversation. Understand?"

"Yes, sir."

"Get back to work."

The restaurant was now in the dinner rush, so Charlene and Gertie didn't get the chance to talk. She did give Gertie a thumbs-up to show that she was still employed, although Gertie could've figured that out from the context clue that Charlene was carrying a full tray into the dining area.

They were both scheduled to work until close. Charlene had a table that was in no hurry to leave, but they were a pleasant couple and it was fine. Around 10:30, she left the dining area, looking forward to soaking her aching body in a bubble bath. Gertie, whose last table had departed twenty minutes ago, was waiting for her.

"So how was your first day?" Charlene asked.

"Third day. It was very interesting."

"This job sucks, right?"

"Nah," said Gertie. "I only cried once. If I can get through an entire shift without stress-vomiting, it's a good job."

"What kind of jobs did you have before this?"

"Customer service."

"Ah. Gotcha."

"Anyway, I wanted to thank you for what you did. You didn't have to do that. You probably shouldn't have done that. You *definitely* shouldn't have done that. But I wanted to thank you the best way I know how."

"Which is?" Charlene asked.

"Alcoholic milkshakes."

"Oh, hell yeah."

"There's a place three blocks away if you're not too tired."

"I was too tired until you said alcoholic milkshakes. Then suddenly my body was filled with a renewed energy, like I could accomplish anything, as long as it involved drinking alcoholic milkshakes."

"Let's go."

They sat at the bar, each with a vanilla milkshake spiked with Bailey's Irish Cream. Gertie had downed the first half of hers at an impressive rate.

"So how long have you been working there?" Gertie asked.

"A few months."

"And you don't need the job?"

"Oh, no. I need the job. I mean, I need *a* job. Earlier today was what I'll call a 'reckless moment.' I'd say that it was the first one, but I'd be lying my ass off. It was maybe, I don't know...reckless moment number twenty thousand, one hundred and eighteen? Twenty thousand, one hundred and nineteen? Something like that. I tend not to do a lot of self-reflection before I act. I feel like you're the opposite."

"Why do you think that?" Gertie asked.

"First impression."

"It's wrong. I'm very impulsive."

"Okay. Good. Give me an example."

"I've got one, but you'll think I'm insane."

"I like insanity. Do tell."

"I'll save it for our second round of shakes," said

Gertie.

"How the hell do you stay that skinny if you drink two milkshakes in a sitting?"

"Lots of walking."

"Fair enough. I'm sticking with one, though."

"You're a cheap date."

"Financially, maybe. Ask my ex-girlfriends about the psychological price."

Gertie laughed. Then she frowned. "Oh, you're—I'm not—I was joking when I called it a date—that's not why I—"

"You're straight. I get it."

"I'm not even bi-curious. Sorry. I didn't—"

"I didn't accept your invite so I could eat your pussy."

Gertie didn't respond to that. The light wasn't very good in here, but Charlene assumed that her cheeks were burning bright red.

"I'm not a predatory lesbian. I'm very much capable of forming bonds with heterosexual women, and am totally cool with the idea that there will be no munching. I assure you, I see you as just a friend and nothing more."

"What if I *was* bi-curious?"

"Still just a friend."

"You complimented my body."

"No, I said you were skinny. And I'd compliment Ryan Reynolds' body if he was sitting next to me. He doesn't get any snatch, either."

"Why just a friend?"

"Are you sure you're only on your first milkshake?"

"It was a very strong milkshake. I should probably only have one. Why just a friend?"

"How many tattoos do you have? None, right?"

"One."

"On your tit?"

"On my ankle."

"A skull?"

"A manatee."

"A manatee with fangs?"

"No."

"See, that's a problem. Are your nipples pierced?"

"Ow. No."

"That's another problem. What am I supposed to jiggle with my tongue? Also, my taste in women runs to those who are emotional black holes. You seem kind of sensitive. And I can tell that you would be a selfish lover. All receiving, no giving in return. Fingers, maybe, but I've got my own fingers."

"I withdraw this whole line of questioning," said Gertie.

"If you ever do decide to play for the other team, I can hook you up, but I'm afraid that our relationship will be forever platonic."

"Sorry if I got weird."

"Not a problem. Weirdness surrounds me."

"Have you always known you were a lesbian?"

"Nope."

"When did you realize it?"

"There was a penis in my mouth at the time."

"I see."

"I liked the guy it was attached to, and I recognized the aesthetic merits of this specific penis—it was very high quality—but it wasn't doing a damn thing for me. I realized I'd been lying to myself about my attraction to guys. Not long after that I decided to act on some strange squishy feelings that I couldn't quite understand, and realized that, yes, this was where I needed to be."

"Did the guy get to finish?"

"I gave him a handy. I'm not a monster."

"Was your family supportive?" Gertie asked.

"Not immediately. It's all good now."

"How long did it take?"

"One thing you should know about me. I will cheerfully tell you that I discovered I like girls while in the midst of a blowjob, but I don't really like to talk about myself all that much. So it's your turn. Give me an example of you being impulsive."

Gertie slurped up the last of her milkshake. "Have you heard about the missing women?"

"Umm, up in Hornbeam Ridge, right? Three or four of them?"

"At least eight in the past few months if you widen the search range. Women who went out by themselves and were never heard from again. Did you know that they all have long dark hair?"

"I did not know that." Charlene's short black hair was as punk rock as she could get away with while working in a family restaurant. Travis had never given her crap about the pink streaks or the way it was shaved on the left side, nor did he object to her nose ring. At the job interview he'd asked if she'd be willing to remove the safety pin from her eyebrow when serving customers because it sent shivers down his spine, and she'd agreed. Gertie had short blonde hair that seemed to be its natural color.

"It's not really making it into the news stories, but I'm sure the police have noticed," said Gertie. "If it's one guy doing this, he has a definite type."

Charlene felt like this conversation might not be headed in a fantastic direction. "Okay," she said. "When you said you were impulsive, I thought you meant in more of a 'drop everything and drive to Vegas' way."

"I haven't told you where I'm going with this."

"You sure haven't."

"One of the missing women is my cousin Kimberly."

"Oh, shit, I'm sorry."

"She disappeared about two months ago. Kimberly is madly in love with her husband and she has two young kids. She'd never just leave. Never."

"It's awful that they have to go through that," said Charlene. "I can't even imagine how I'd handle the not knowing part."

"So I've been walking the streets of Hornbeam Ridge at night, wearing a wig with long brown hair, trying to catch the guy who did it."

They each ordered another milkshake.

"Explain to me exactly what you're doing," said Charlene. "Because, no judgment, but you were right when you said I'd think you were insane."

"I'm well aware that it's not one hundred percent sane," said Gertie.

"So explain."

"I have a stun gun and also a real gun. Every couple of nights I've been driving out to Hornbeam Ridge, putting on the wig, and walking around town for hours, hoping he'll come after me. If he does, he'll get a nasty surprise."

"Let me get this straight," said Charlene. "You walk around after dark, wearing a...you know what, I don't need to summarize what you said. You know how it sounds."

"I have a permit for the gun."

"That wasn't my first question."

"And I'm fast on the draw with the stun gun. If he came after me, I know I could defend myself. He'd be lying on the sidewalk in a puddle of his own piss, and the cops would force him to take them to the missing women."

"What if he had a gun, too? What would you do if he just pointed a gun at you and said, 'Get in the trunk of my car, bitch,'?"

"I've been following the stories. You can't kidnap eight different people—at least—by just pointing guns at them and giving instructions. He had to lure them somehow."

"Or jump out at them from the shadows."

"I'm careful."

"Oh, yeah, you sound like The Amazing Ms. Caution. During the day, she gives safety lessons to young schoolchildren. At night, she's fucked in the head."

"It's not a foolproof plan. But I'm not going to just hang out at home and wait for the cops to catch this guy. Not when I could be doing my part."

"How do you know it's a guy?"

"I don't. But when eight women with long dark hair are abducted, I tend to assume that the kidnapper is a dude."

"Makes sense."

"And it doesn't matter. I'll zap a chick, too."

The bartender set their milkshakes on the counter in front of them.

"I'll be honest," said Charlene. "I thought that me referencing pussy eating would be the most uncomfortable part of our talk."

"So you see how I'm impulsive."

"Um, no. You arm yourself and walk around a designated area with a specific goal in mind. It's kind of the opposite of impulsive. Dangerous, yes. Whack-adoodle crazy, you betcha. Suicidal? Close. But not impulsive."

"It's not a designated area. I just go around where other victims were last seen."

"Okay, the whole impulsive vs. non-impulsive thing doesn't matter," said Charlene. "What does matter is that you should not be wandering the streets at night trying to draw the attention of somebody who could be a serial killer."

"I disagree."

"I get that we just met tonight, and that our primary interaction was you watching me make a poor decision at work. I'm not a good source of advice. I'm actually a terrible source of advice. But I don't have to be a genius to say 'Don't do shit like that.' Have you told anybody else? Your parents? Your cousin's husband?"

"No."

"Why not?"

"Because."

"Because they'd tell you not to do shit like that."

"Right."

"It's top-notch advice."

"I know it is," Charlene admitted. "But what am I supposed to do? Put up signs? Post on social media? Ask for thoughts and prayers?"

"Yes. All of those things. Except the thoughts and prayers."

"Well, I didn't expect you to understand. I was just making conversation. You're right—it's not impulsive. But it's also not stupid or suicidal. Yeah, it's dangerous, but I know how to defend myself, and I won't hesitate to put myself in danger to try to rescue somebody I love. Kimberly has a family. If it's too late to get her back, at least I can try to make sure it doesn't happen to anybody else."

Charlene suddenly felt like kind of a jerk for calling her insane. Not that she thought she was *wrong*—she just felt bad for saying it. Who knew what she would do if somebody she cared about went missing?

"That makes sense," Charlene said. "Are you going over there tonight?"

"Not after two booze shakes, no. I try to stay sober when I prowl the streets hunting for a serial kidnapper."

"I'm glad to hear that."

"Tomorrow night, though."

The way Gertie looked at Charlene made her uncomfortable, like she was hinting at a favor.

"I'm not coming with you," said Charlene.

"I didn't ask you to."

"I know, but I got that vibe."

Gertie shook her head. "I literally am not asking you to come with me. The women were alone when they went missing. If I walk the streets with somebody, he won't come after me. You'd ruin the whole plan. And we'd have to buy another wig. Those aren't cheap. We couldn't get it over your spiky hair, and brown hair doesn't really go with your complexion, so that could spoil the ruse."

"My hair wouldn't be an issue," said Charlene. "Everything else makes sense."

"Sorry. I've gotta go solo."

"I wasn't offering to join you."

"You sounded like you wanted to come."

"I specifically said no. I was even rude about it."

"Well, you can't come."

"I know. We've established this."

Gertie peered at her glass. "I think they put more Bailey's in my milkshake than usual."

"That's very possible. I still say you're out of your mind, but I'll also say that you're a good, caring person. And brave."

"Are you hitting on me?"

"Nope. Not into sloppy drunks."

"I'm buzzed, not drunk. And I haven't spilt anything. You're the sloppy one, Dr. Lasagna."

"That was done on your behalf."

Gertie smiled. "Uh-huh."

"Are you questioning that?"

"Maybe a little."

"She made you cry. You were crying in the back room because of the way a customer treated you. Actual tears."

"Did you *see* her treat me badly?"

"No. Holy crap, did you set me up?"

"Oh, no, no, no, no. She was horrible to me. I'm just saying that you didn't see the interaction and you didn't know me. Maybe all she did was get a little snippy. Maybe I was a crybaby. Maybe this was the third time I'd forgotten to bring her the butter she asked for and she'd reached a breaking point. Maybe I was crying because I'd broken up with my boyfriend and I lied to you because I was a pathological liar. All I'm saying is that on some level, you were happy to have an excuse to dump pasta on a customer."

"You know what, I completely agree with your psychoanalysis," said Charlene.

"Really? Because while I was saying it I thought it made me sound ungrateful."

"Oh, you definitely sounded ungrateful. But I agree with your assessment. I'm a crazy bitch who'll dump

29

pasta on a customer who might be wrongfully accused, and you're a crazy bitch who'll walk the streets searching for a dangerous psychopath."

Gertie lifted her milkshake glass. "Here's to being two crazy bitches."

They clinked their glasses together.

"Can you imagine the sex we'd have?" asked Charlene.

Gertie laughed. "Crazy bitch sex? Is that safe? Shouldn't one partner be the sane one? I feel like you need a voice of reason or else you end up, I don't know, like, using habanero peppers as sex toys."

"I draw the line at candle wax."

"I draw the line at 'ouch.'"

"Yeah, we definitely wouldn't be compatible."

"At least we can be friends, though."

"We can definitely be friends," said Charlene.

"I don't think I should drive right now. So I was going to just sit on this stool for a while and talk to whomever is sitting next to me. Do you want to be that person?"

"Sure, why not?"

CHAPTER THREE

The other woman wasn't dead yet. Olivia could hear her breathing.

None of the other women in the cages had made any sounds since Olivia first woke up and found herself here. With no windows and no way to calculate the passage of time, Olivia couldn't be sure how long she'd been locked up, but she didn't think it had been a full day yet.

Since she barely had any room in the cage to move, her body had begun to ache, which turned to excruciating pain, which eventually gave way to numbness. Now she couldn't feel anything. This meant that if she *did* get loose, she'd just collapse onto the floor, unable to move. Not that it mattered. It had been several hours since she'd believed there was a way to escape the cage.

A sound behind her. A doorknob turning? She tried to turn her head to look behind her but her muscles weren't cooperating.

She heard a door open, then close. Followed by a fingernails-against-a-chalkboard screech. The sound got closer and closer until she finally saw Greg, either clean shaven or no longer wearing a fake beard, dragging the wooden chair across the concrete floor. The bandage on his neck was gone, revealing no cut. He had a brown paper bag in his free hand. He placed the chair a few feet in front of her cage, then sat down in it. He looked up at her. He stood up, adjusted the position of the chair, and sat down again.

"*Please*—" Olivia said.

"No," said Greg. "No begging. No pleading." He gestured to the other cages. "It didn't work for the other girls, and it's not going to work for you. Don't ask me what I want. Don't ask me why I'm doing this. Don't offer me anything. If I wanted to rape you, I would've done it before I locked you up there."

"I have to pee."

"I'm not going to let you out to pee. You know that. I can see from the floor that you weren't able to hold it before I got here. Don't worry about me having to clean up. Do what you need to do."

"Please. People will be looking for me."

Greg shrugged. "So? I didn't snatch some crack whore from behind a Dumpster. Of course people will be looking for you. I enjoy that part. I get to watch their sad faces on television. Who will be the most heartbroken that you're gone? Your mother? Father? Boyfriend? Children?"

"I left clues."

"No, you didn't. I'm not sure you even knew what planet you were on. Like I said, these other girls tried every trick in the book, and having you just regurgitate what they did is kind of pissing me off." He scooted the chair a bit to the left. "Not that it matters. Your fate is the same no matter what you do. Nothing you can do will change it. Imagine that you've leapt off the top of a hundred-story skyscraper and you're plummeting toward the pavement. The only possible ending in that scenario is you splattered on the ground. The only possible ending here is with you starving to death in that cage. Like the rest of them."

He stood up and walked over to the cage next to Olivia's. He gave it a gentle shove. The woman opened her eyes.

"Oh, good, you're still alive. Maybe I'll get lucky and you'll succumb before I have to leave."

The woman said nothing.

Greg returned his attention to Olivia. "Want to hear something that's going to really upset you? I almost had to let you go. Seriously. You kept watching your drink. If that lady hadn't stumbled over to the table and distracted you, I wouldn't have taken the chance. You may have thought that she was my accomplice, but nope, it was just terrible luck on your part. One drunken fan praising your set and now you're up there. Life is pretty strange."

Olivia had no reaction to that revelation. At this point, she didn't care about irony.

Greg opened the brown bag and took out a bottle of water and a straw. "I know that accepting a drink from me didn't work out for you last time," he said, "but I promise you, this is just water." He set the bottle on the chair then walked out of sight.

More screeching across the floor. He was strong enough to just pick up a stepladder, so Olivia assumed he was making the ghastly noise on purpose. He set the ladder next to the other woman's cage, then picked up the bottle and climbed up to her cage. "I'm watering her first because she's closer to death," he explained.

33

He held the bottle out to the woman. She leaned her head forward and began to suck through the straw.

"Slow down," Greg told her. "You don't want to make yourself sick."

The woman didn't slow down. Then she coughed and threw up the water, which splashed all over the floor.

"Slower this time," he said.

She waved him away. Greg climbed down the ladder and moved it next to Olivia's cage. He took a second bottle of water out of the bag, unscrewed the cap, and put in the same straw he'd used in the other woman's bottle. He placed his foot on the bottom rung of the ladder, then looked up at Olivia.

"I can't stop you from trying something stupid," he said. "Just know that it means you won't get any water."

"I won't try anything," said Olivia.

"Good." Greg climbed up the ladder and extended the bottle to Olivia. She forced herself to drink slowly. Greg waited patiently as she finished off the entire bottle of cold water. "Want the rest of Regina's?" he asked.

Olivia shook her head. The odds of successfully kicking him off the ladder, causing him to shatter his skull against the floor, were extremely low. She still would've tried—she just couldn't get her legs to move.

Greg climbed back down. He dragged the ladder out of the way, then sat down in his chair. He took out a cell phone, quickly glanced at the display, then shoved it back into his pocket.

"I'd like you to do me a favor and be quiet for a while," he said. "If you want to cry or whimper, that's okay, but don't talk, all right?"

Olivia didn't respond.

Greg just sat there, silently staring at the women in

cages. Every once in a while there'd be a hint of a smile, but mostly his expression was blank.

It felt like about half an hour before he did anything else. He took his cell phone out again, tapped the screen as if sending a text message, then pocketed it, looking annoyed.

He glanced back up at Olivia. "When I told you I enjoyed your music, I was lying, but it wasn't complete bullshit. You've got some talent. You were never going to be a superstar, but if I was a real manager I probably could've gotten you into a bigger club. If it will make you feel better to sing, go ahead and sing a couple of songs. Entertain me."

No way was Olivia going to sing for him. She'd let him rip out her vocal cords with his teeth first.

She wanted to tell him to go to hell. She settled for gently shaking her head.

Greg pointed to the cage next to hers. "Do it for your neighbor, then. She hasn't had any entertainment for the past few days except watching me put you up there. Sing her a song. Upbeat, depressing, I don't care. Sing something."

"No."

"What's wrong? Don't like the acoustics in this venue?" Greg laughed far too hard at his own joke. "C'mon, sing for us. Before too long you won't have the energy. Give the world one last song."

"Go to hell."

Greg stood up. "I bet if I broke one of your fingers you'd sing. Your pitch would go up a couple of octaves but you'd sing." He glanced over at Regina. "Hey, is she dead?"

He walked over and poked Regina's leg. She didn't

respond. He jabbed at her with his index finger a few more times, until finally she opened her eyes.

"Ah, okay, still around. Couldn't see you breathing."

Regina closed her eyes again. Greg sat back down.

"I'm not going to break one of your fingers," he told Olivia. "I'm better than that now. I'm just going to watch. If you want to sing, sing. If you don't, don't. Your choice."

He leaned back, stretched out his legs, and stared at her.

Olivia wanted to close her eyes so she wouldn't have to look at him, but she was too frightened. She didn't want to open her eyes and discover him standing right next to her cage, reaching for her foot. And she didn't want to fall asleep. Falling asleep with him in the room should've been impossible, but her energy level was extremely low and she felt like she could indeed lose consciousness if she kept her eyes closed for too long.

So they watched each other.

For hours.

He shifted positions every once in a while and took stretch breaks, but for the most part he just sat there, motionless, watching.

Finally he checked his phone once more, scowled, and carried the chair back across the room. He tried to give Regina some more water, but she wouldn't drink. Olivia drank half of another bottle. Though her bladder felt like it was ready to explode—and she would let it burst before she urinated in front of him—it seemed like he was getting ready to depart and she could relieve herself after he left the room.

"Thank you for spending the evening with me," he said. "I'll be back soon."

He left.

Seconds after the door closed, Olivia peed her pants again, and then sobbed.

Kenneth Dove (not Greg the talent manager, not Christopher the model scout, not Jack with car trouble, or any of the others) pulled off to the side of the road before turning onto his street. He rolled down the window, then opened the glove compartment and took out a bottle of Jack Daniels. He poured some into his mouth, swished it around for a moment, then spat it out the window. He dabbed some onto his fingers and wiped them on his shirt. He'd changed into his smoke-scented shirt before getting in the car.

He rolled his window back up, put away the bottle, and drove the rest of the way home.

As he opened the front door, he was greeted by the scent of absolutely no dinner on the table. Vivian walked into the living room. Not surprisingly, she looked pissed.

"Seriously?" she asked.

Ken stepped inside. "Don't jump on my ass the second I walk through the door. I had to work late."

"Uh-huh." Vivian gave him one of the nasty glares she'd perfected over the past seventeen years. "You're not fooling anybody. I know exactly where you were."

"Whatever."

"*Whatever*," she mimicked. "You sound like a teenager. Speaking of which, he got in trouble again at school."

"What'd he do this time?"

"Why don't you ask him?"

"So I don't even get five minutes of peace after working late? I've gotta go straight to disciplinarian?"

"You know, Ken, when you act like I'm stupid, it really hurts my feelings. It really does. It makes me feel like you don't care about me."

"Oh, jeez, I'm sorry. I'm just tired." Ken walked over to Vivian and put his arms around her. He gave her a gentle kiss on the lips and ran his fingers through her long blonde hair. She recoiled a bit at the whiskey on his breath but didn't say anything. "You're the smartest girl I know."

"Then maybe start treating me that way."

"I will, I promise." He gave her a tight hug. Then he called over her shoulder. "Jared! C'mon down here!"

It took about thirty seconds before he heard the sound of footsteps clomping down the stairs. Jared walked into the living room. The kid was huge, and at sixteen hadn't stopped growing yet. He could've easily gotten a football scholarship, but he had no interest in sports. Or academics. Or anything besides video games and a series of slutty girlfriends. (Vivian, bless her oblivious heart, didn't know he was actually screwing them in his bedroom. About two years ago, Ken had sat Jared down for a very serious father/son talk. Good ol' Dad would pretend not to know what was going on, but if Jared was careless enough to get one of them pregnant, he was on his own.)

"What's up?" Jared asked.

"You tell me," said Ken, letting go of Vivian. "I hear you had an interesting day at school."

Jared shrugged.

"Your mom is right here. I mean, literally standing here in this very room. So pretending that you don't know what I'm talking about is disrespectful to her."

"It was a stupid test anyway."

"Give me more information than that."

"I cheated on my math test."

"Jesus Christ, Jared."

"I don't need to know any of this stuff. It's not helping me out with life."

"Did you get suspended?"

"Nah," said Jared. "Just got a zero. It wasn't even a test, it was a quiz."

"Oh, well, shit, if it was only a quiz it's no big deal, right? Surely cheating on a quiz is worth having a great big blotch on your permanent record. You don't need college, right? That's just a silly little place where people earn silly little degrees that help them get good jobs. But you're going to be one of those millionaire video game players. My God, a universe of career opportunities awaits you with that astounding hand-eye coordination of yours! Your mom and I have already picked out the mansion you're gonna buy us. It's got three swimming pools. Three! All of those colleges that reject your application because you're a cheater sure are going to feel dumb when they see what an amazing success you've made of yourself."

Jared looked at the floor. "Okay, I get it."

"No, I don't think you do. Because I'm going to destroy your career potential. You're going to march upstairs, and you're going to disconnect your PlayStation, and you're going to bring it down here, and I'm going to lock it up for the next two weeks, and you're not going to give me any attitude about it. And if this happens again, I'm going to get a hammer out of the garage and I'm going to smash your beloved game to pieces. I don't just mean cheating; I mean any trouble at school. You hear me?"

"Yeah."

"You think 'yeah' is gonna cut it?"

"Yes, sir."

"Go up there and get it. And don't you dare try to finish the level that you're on."

Jared left the living room.

"There," said Ken to Vivian. "Parental duties fulfilled."

Ken and Vivian sat up in bed, watching television. Vivian reached under the covers and slid her hand over his crotch.

"Looking for something?" he asked.

She smiled. "I bet it'll get easier to find in a minute."

Vivian rubbed on him for far more than a minute, but nothing was happening. It wasn't that she lacked skill—she was, in fact, quite talented with her fingers. And he recognized that she was still attractive. She kept in shape and was only about ten pounds heavier than when they first met. (She'd been quite a bit heavier at their wedding, but she'd been eight months pregnant with Jared.) Vivian was attractive in a purely objective sense, just not attractive to him anymore. It was like that thing he'd seen online with a half-naked, absolutely gorgeous girl on her hands and knees giving a come-hither look to the camera, with the caption, "*No matter how hot she is, somebody out there is tired of putting up with her shit.*"

He was tired of putting up with Vivian's shit.

Had been for years.

But, points for trying. She was, after all, initiating sex. And it wasn't worth the trouble of saying that he was exhausted, or just not in the mood.

He closed his eyes and thought of the women in cages.

Thought of the first one to die, who had very little skin left now.

Thought of Regina, who might no longer be breathing.

Thought of poor Olivia, maybe the only one left alive in that room. Hanging in a cage with all those rotting corpses. So scared. So pretty. All of them were beautiful.

"Now that's more like it," said Vivian.

They got completely undressed and he mounted her.

Ken fantasized about emaciated, caged women as he fucked the shit out of his wife.

CHAPTER FOUR

"You won't believe the dream I had last night," Gertie told Charlene the next day, as they got ready to begin their shift.

"Was I in it?"

"Yes."

"Was it kinky?"

"No."

"Was I a mermaid?"

"I should probably just tell you."

"That might be better."

"We were walking the streets of Hornbeam Ridge together. You kept saying that it was a bad idea, but in the dream he'd kidnapped your sister, and—"

"I don't have a sister," said Charlene.

"In my nocturnal landscape, you had a sister."

"Okay."

"You kept saying it was a bad idea, but then you said the reason we weren't finding him is that we weren't looking in scary enough places. And it made sense. If we were tracking a psychopath, we wouldn't look in well-lit areas, we'd look in scary places."

"Dream logic."

"And you said there was this door that everybody in the neighborhood knew about and nobody knew where it went. So you led me there, and there were trees with messed-up faces all around it, and we could hear people screaming on the other side."

"My God, that was no dream!"

"Shut up. We got the door open, I forget how, and it basically led to Hell. And my cousin Kimberly and your sister and all of the other women were there, floating on this pier in a lake of lava, tied up with serpents. I knew it was them even though none of them had faces. And we both knew that we could've just turned around and walked back out that door. I know this because I could hear your thoughts. But we didn't. Somehow we could tell that the lava wouldn't burn us, maybe because we didn't belong there, so we swam out to the pier and untied the snakes. Then Satan showed up and I woke up."

"That's a very interesting dream you had there," said Charlene.

"I know, right?"

"Is it coincidence that you met me and now you're having dreams about the devil?"

"My takeaway from the dream is that you were willing to follow me into Hell."

Travis stepped into the back room and tapped his wrist where a watch would be if he were wearing one. Normally Charlene would make a wise-ass remark, but after yesterday she thought she should be on her best behavior for a few days.

Breaks were staggered, and it was an insanely busy night, so they didn't get to resume their conversation until shortly before closing time. Charlene still had a couple of tables when Gertie clocked out.

"Any plans for tonight?" Charlene asked.

"Nah."

"You sure?"

"Nothing like what you're talking about," said Gertie. "I have a date with Netflix, sweatpants, and Chinese carryout."

"You don't have to lie to me."

"I'm not lying."

"One of my skills, and I have many, is that I can tell when people are lying. So when you avoid eye contact, even though all you're doing is telling me about a pleasant evening at home, I have to assume that you're headed out to use yourself as bait."

"All right, busted."

"Why would you lie about that?" Charlene asked.

"Because I'm kind of embarrassed that I told you in the first place. It makes me sound...less than completely stable."

"It does. I'm not going to spare your feelings and pretend it doesn't. However, I've been thinking about it for this whole shift, and I'd like to help you."

"Wait, what?"

"I'm serious."

"Is one of your other skills messing with people?"

"It is, but not right now. I think what you're doing is dangerous and misguided but it comes from a good place, and I want to help keep you safe."

"We can't stick together, though. Only one woman has gone missing at a time. There'd be safety in numbers, and even if he does see us, he'll probably leave us alone."

"Oh, I'm not offering to walk with you. That's just

nuts. What I will do is drive around the area where you are, parking at different places for a few minutes at a time."

"He might be looking out for possible witnesses, though. If he sees you sitting in a car, that might be enough to keep him away."

"I won't be within sight of you. We'll keep in touch through text messages. If you don't check in every, say, five minutes, I'll know something's wrong. It's not much, but it's better than you going missing and nobody knowing about it until you don't show up at work."

"I actually really like that plan," said Gertie.

"Let me be clear. If you get into trouble, I'm calling the police. I'm not rushing out there to help try to overpower the guy. That's all on you. But I'll be your, I don't know, protector from a distance."

"That sounds great. I really appreciate it."

"And then you have to buy me drinks when we're done."

"Deal."

"When were you heading out?"

"Right after I go home and get changed. Do you want to go back to my place?"

"Are you—"

"I said that and immediately knew it was a setup for a lesbian comment."

"I'll save the comment for your next setup. Yes, I'd like to go back to your place for some platonic undressing."

As Charlene pulled into the parking lot of Gertie's apartment complex, she was surprised by how excited she was. She shouldn't be excited. This was absolute madness that could end horribly. Not that Charlene thought Gertie would actually draw out the culprit, but plenty of other things could go wrong when an attractive young woman walked by herself after dark. And if Charlene couldn't even watch her, she wasn't providing that much protection.

Still, it was better than nothing. And what if by some miracle they *did* capture the piece of shit and help the police find those missing women? That would be unbelievable.

Though Charlene knew it wouldn't work out like that, she still couldn't get rid of the feeling of excitement. She'd had a great many wild experiences in her lifetime, but this was a brand new addition to her resume. It wouldn't be *fun*—not with lives at stake—but it would be interesting. Very, very interesting.

Gertie got out of her own car, and they walked up the stairs to Gertie's apartment together. "Just to warn you," she said, inserting her key into the lock, "I'm a total neat freak. You're going to see organization and tidiness that may make you uncomfortable, so I apologize in advance."

"Are you saying that you think I'm a slob?"

"I get a 'dirty clothes on the floor' vibe from you."

"I'll have you know that I scrub the grout on my bathroom floor every single morning with a toothbrush."

"Uh-huh."

"Okay, yes, there are dirty clothes on the floor and clutter everywhere. Does that fit into your stereotype of lesbians?"

"I have no idea what the stereotype is for lesbian housekeeping."

"I don't think there is one. Gay guys have one but we don't."

Gertie opened the door and they walked into her apartment.

"Holy crap," said Charlene. "You weren't kidding."

"I warned you."

"You've color-coordinated your books."

"Yep. And they're alphabetized by author within the color coordination."

Charlene walked over to the bookcase. "That is some serial killer behavior right there. Where do you keep your notebooks filled with tiny print?"

"I'll just be a minute," said Gertie, walking into her bedroom and closing the door.

Charlene wandered around the living room. She wondered if Gertie would notice if she slid the coaster on the coffee table a half-inch to the right, and decided that she probably would. Charlene didn't test this theory.

Gertie's Blu-Ray collection, mostly independent cinema, passed muster. Apparently all of her music was digital, so Charlene would wait to pass judgment upon her collection. Her reading habits were all over the place. Charlene was tempted to peek in her refrigerator or medicine cabinet, but that kind of snooping was only acceptable if she'd had sex with the person.

Gertie came out of her bedroom, wearing jeans, a sweater, and a light jacket. She also wore a wig to give her long brown hair. It wasn't a flattering look for her facial structure, so it was good that she was trying to lure a psychopath instead of get a boyfriend.

"Do you have a gun right now?" Charlene asked.

"Yes."

"Oh. Okay, well, guns make me really nervous, so don't, like, fall or anything."

"I won't fall down on my gun." Gertie reached into her jacket pocket and took out the stun gun. She pressed a button and Charlene could see the electricity crackle between the two electrodes.

"I didn't realize you could actually see the electricity on those things," she said. "I thought that was a special effect in movies."

"Nope. I've got an extra one for you."

"No, that's okay. I won't be leaving my car."

"You sure?"

"Positive. Stun guns, real guns, nail guns—they all freak me out. But I'm glad you have them. Shall we be off?"

They got into Charlene's car. As they drove away, Charlene realized that she was more nervous around guns than she'd thought. Just knowing that Gertie had one concealed somewhere was making it difficult to focus on her driving. She'd once done sex play that involved a switchblade knife (but only once) so she wasn't completely weapons-phobic, but damn, she hated having that gun in the car.

"Okay, every five minutes I'll check in with you," said Gertie. "Just a quick one-word text. People are on their phones all the time when they walk, so I don't think that will scare him away if he sees me doing it, but I also don't want him to think that I'm in the middle of a conversation where somebody will notice right away if I stop responding."

"That works. You get thirty seconds of grace period. If I don't get a response by then, I'm calling 911."

"Let's make it at least a minute."

"Why?"

"Because thirty seconds is too short."

"Why?"

"Because if I notice that somebody is watching me, I don't want to spook him by suddenly taking out my phone. There may be a situation where I have to play it cool, and having a thirty-second ticking clock could mess everything up."

"If it's him watching you, don't you want the police to be on their way as soon as possible?"

"What if it's not him?"

"Then don't shoot him."

"I don't want you to call in a false alarm. Give me five extra minutes if I don't respond."

"No. In five minutes you could be in an alley with your ribcage cracked open."

"Two minutes."

"I get what you're saying, but I will be haunted forever if I go along with this plan and you get abducted or killed or both. So I am not going to just wait if something seems to be wrong. If that's a problem, I'm out."

Gertie stared out the window for a moment. "All right. You're the one giving up her evening for me. I will make every effort to respond in thirty seconds, and if you have to call 911, that's fine. Anyway, we both know that there's almost zero chance that I'll actually encounter this guy."

"I knew that. I'm glad you know that."

Gertie lowered the visor and checked herself out in the small mirror. "Does this look work for me?"

"You look better as a blonde."

"Yeah, I think so, too. Actually, the color is fine, but

hair this straight doesn't work with my face." She raised the visor again. "I'm not sure if I mentioned this yesterday, but this whole idea terrifies me. I may have given the impression that I'm brave and casual about it, and that's wrong. I'm scared shitless. So unless you think it's really rude, I'm just going to sit here with my eyes closed and do deep-breathing exercises until we get there."

"That's totally cool."

"Thank you." Gertie closed her eyes.

Charlene wondered if this was a bad idea. Then she wondered why she was wondering—of *course* this was a bad idea. It was a terrible idea. It was a ridiculous idea. The fact that this was a bad idea was never in question. It was the kind of thing a guy would do hoping to get laid.

Her friendship with Gertie was still in the "budding" stage, but she enjoyed her company and didn't want to see her get hurt.

She'd only be doing this once, though.

She'd forgotten to ask if she could turn on the radio before Gertie began her deep breathing, and didn't know if that would mess up her efforts to go to her happy place before offering herself up to an abductor, so Charlene drove in silence.

About half an hour later, she pulled into the parking lot of a convenience store. This already seemed like the kind of place where you could get murdered after dark. Charlene shut off the engine.

"Every five minutes," she told Gertie.

Gertie nodded. "Thank you for this."

"Thank me after you end up not dismembered."

"Morbid humor isn't really what I need right now."

"It's what you get. Are you sure you want to do this? I

bet we could find a late-night sushi place. Go to a movie. Knock on a stranger's door and offer to reorganize their bookshelves."

Gertie opened the car door. "I'm heading north. I'll let you know if anything changes. Just sort of keep heading in that direction."

"All right. Please be careful."

"I will."

"Be constantly aware of my therapy bill if this goes bad."

"I'm trying to save my cousin."

"I know, I know. I apologize. Good luck."

Gertie got out of the car, shut the door, and walked off.

This was suddenly not as exciting as Charlene had thought it might be. Her stomach twisted itself into knots like Christmas lights when you pulled them out of storage. She needed a Xanax.

Everything would be fine. Gertie had already done this dumb shit many times without getting hurt, so she'd be fine tonight, too.

It was five minutes after eleven. Gertie had been gone for one minute. Charlene could still see her. It was too early to check in.

Charlene scrolled through Instagram for four minutes, then sent Gertie a text.

Still alive?

The answer came back right away: *Yep.* ☺

Charlene played on her phone for another five minutes.

How's it going?

Fine.

It was probably time to move to a new parking spot. Charlene turned on the engine, wondering how she was going to make it through the next couple of hours without having a nervous breakdown.

Gertie kept her hand inside of her pocket, fingers wrapped around the stun gun.

She honestly didn't know if she wanted to find the guy or not. She wanted to save Kimberly and the other missing women, and she relished the idea of sending 150,000 volts into the body of the son of a bitch who'd taken them. She didn't relish the idea of being bound and gagged in the trunk of a car. She didn't relish the idea of him stroking her hair as he whispered the wicked things he was going to do to her. She didn't relish the idea of him taking his time with the knife, because there was nobody around to hear her scream.

But she couldn't sit at home and do nothing. The cops hadn't caught this guy. They didn't even have any leads, as far as she knew. She didn't genuinely believe that she'd be the one to bring him to justice, but it helped her sleep at night to know she was at least trying.

Her phone buzzed. She texted back *OK* to Charlene and tucked the phone away again.

She didn't feel that much safer, but it was nice to know that somebody was with her on this weird scheme, even if Charlene thought she was mentally ill.

Gertie checked in every five minutes. Nothing happened to make her delay by even a few seconds. In fact, she was hardly seeing anybody out tonight. A couple of joggers. A lady walking her dog. An old man who informed her that she shouldn't be out alone at night—there was a madman on the loose.

She'd been out for almost an hour. Maybe she should quit for the night. She felt bad that Charlene was just sitting in a car, waiting for updates. This was a pretty damn big favor from somebody she'd just met. And technically, Charlene wasn't in her debt, she was in Charlene's debt for the lasagna vengeance.

She wasn't going to catch anybody tonight.

She knew that.

She should just go home. Or out for sushi. Though the alcoholic milkshakes had been expensive and she couldn't really afford sushi until payday. So she should just go home.

Maybe in another ten minutes.

Less than ten minutes later, she saw a man walking toward her. He was holding the hand of a little boy, maybe six years old. The boy had a teddy bear and a couple of balloons.

Why was a kid this young out after midnight?

The man avoided eye contact as Gertie walked past them. And he looked kind of nervous.

The kid didn't seem scared, though.

Still, the teddy bear looked brand new. And why would the kid have balloons? A child's birthday party wouldn't end this late.

It was probably completely innocent, but it didn't seem right. Gertie took out her phone and called Charlene.

"What's up?" Charlene asked.

"Could you do me a quick favor?" Gertie asked. "Could you check for an AMBER Alert in this area? It would be a five or six-year-old boy with black hair. With a man in his thirties, also black hair, glasses."

"Do you know the license plate?"

"They're walking."

"Okay, sure."

"I'm going to follow them."

"Are you—"

"Yes, I'm sure it's a good idea. Let me know as soon as possible. Thanks."

Gertie turned around and walked after the man and child. If they looked back, they might wonder why she'd changed direction, but if nothing criminal was going on they had nothing to worry about. They certainly wouldn't think that she was going to mug them.

She wasn't sure how far back to stay. She didn't want to raise suspicion, but she didn't want to lose them. Gertie had no experience in trying to follow somebody; one turn and she might not be able to find them again.

They turned right at the next corner.

Shit.

Gertie picked up her pace.

Her phone vibrated. "Yeah?" she whispered.

"No active AMBER Alerts around here."

"Doesn't mean the kid wasn't kidnapped, though."

"What exactly did you see?"

"It's a man walking with a little kid. The kid has balloons and a teddy bear. I know that doesn't sound like much, but—"

"—but it's midnight. I get it. You think the kid was bribed with gifts?"

"Maybe. I mean, parents are allowed to have their kids out late. I got a weird vibe from him is all."

"I'm pretty sure an AMBER Alert only goes out if the

kid is in physical danger. Call 911 and see if there have been any reports."

Gertie turned the corner. She hadn't lost the man and boy yet.

"I will," she whispered. "Stay put. I'll call you back."

Charlene's stomach had somehow twisted into even tighter knots. There were plenty of reasons a man might be out this late with a balloon-holding little kid. She had no idea what time Chuck E. Cheese closed. Could be a divorced dad who had to drive several hours after work to pick up his son for visitation. "Child abduction" was one of the less likely explanations.

And suppose it *was* an abduction. The guy wasn't going to turn around and kidnap Gertie, too. She'd call the police and let them do their jobs.

Gertie, who did not have her own ringtone yet, called.

"I need you to pick me up right away," said Gertie, sounding panicked and out of breath. "They went into a parking garage."

"Where?"

"It's...no, don't pick me up in the garage. There's a café called Four Umbrellas. GPS it and pick me up right outside of it. I'm switching back to 911. Bye."

Charlene quickly pulled up the café on her phone. Only a few blocks away.

A couple of blocks later she stopped at a red light. There was no other traffic, so she went ahead and ran it. If a cop pulled her over, that'd be a *good* thing, right?

Gertie stood outside of the café. There was street

parking right in front of it, so Charlene pulled up alongside the sidewalk and Gertie got into the car.

"They haven't come out yet," Gertie said. "Looks like there's only one exit, so we'll see them."

"What's going on?"

"A dad who was denied custody took his kid. Beat the shit out of the mother before he left. She literally called the cops a couple of minutes before I did. We can't let him get away."

CHAPTER FIVE

"Okay, all right," said Charlene. "Do you know for sure that he's getting in a car? The parking garage could be connected to another building or something."

Gertie shook her head. "All I know is that he went in there with the little boy. I assume he's getting in a car."

"Then we'll wait. We can wait. That's no problem. He'll pull out right in front of us, we'll get a description of his vehicle, hopefully get the license plate, and pass that on to the police. Easy."

"And then we're going to follow them," said Gertie.

"Right. Yes. Of course. We'll follow them from a safe distance."

"Unless you have to bash the car off the road."

"I'm the one who's supposed to make inappropriate jokes," said Charlene.

"That wasn't a joke. If we have to stop him from getting away, you may have to bash the car off the road." Gertie fastened her seat belt. "Don't worry. It'll be a last resort. And they aren't going to raise your insurance rates if you did it to save a child."

"I wasn't worried about my insurance rates. I was worried about death."

"We're not gonna die."

"I know, I know, I know. Shit." Charlene took a deep breath. "Okay, I'm totally focused now. The son of a bitch isn't going to get away. But promise me you aren't going to start shooting through windows and stuff."

"I'm not."

"Swear to me. I don't want you getting caught up in the heat of the moment and opening fire and accidentally killing an innocent little kid. If they get away, they get away. No gunfire."

"I'm not going to shoot the kid."

"My point is that you might try to shoot out their tires and hit the kid. We will follow them. But don't start shooting. In fact, throw your gun in the backseat."

The gate lifted and a silver car pulled out of the parking garage. Charlene could see a couple of balloons floating in the back seat.

"That's them! That's them!" said Gertie. She put the phone to her ear. "It's a silver car. Two-door. I don't know the model—no, wait, it's turning around. There's a Chevrolet logo on the back. No license plate." She waved to Charlene. "Go, go!"

Charlene pulled back onto the road and followed the silver car. It was going thirty-five, the speed limit. This might not be so bad.

"We're headed east," said Gertie into the phone. "Just passed 12th Street."

The car stopped at a red light. Charlene stopped directly behind it.

Did the guy suspect that he was being followed? What would he do if he figured it out?

"We're right behind him," said Gertie.

Charlene wiped some perspiration from her forehead. Her underarms were soaked. Maybe Gertie *should* shoot out the car's tires. It wasn't moving right now.

No, no, no, no, no. The guy could come after them. Or hurt the kid. That was an astoundingly bad idea and Charlene was glad that she hadn't suggested it. Gertie didn't reach for her gun, so the astoundingly bad idea probably hadn't occurred to her.

The light turned green and the car went through the intersection. Charlene followed.

"Let him get ahead a little bit," said Gertie. "We don't want him to know we're following him."

"How close are the police?"

Gertie asked the same question to whomever she was speaking to on the phone. After a moment, she looked at Charlene. "They're on their way. Shouldn't be long."

A siren sounded off in the distance.

Gertie smiled. "Not long at all."

The silver car sped up, rocketing forward and running a yellow light.

"Shit!" said Charlene.

"He's speeding off!"

"I see that!"

"Follow him!"

Charlene floored the gas pedal. The light was now red and she cringed as she sped through the intersection, waiting for another car to plow into her. Fortunately, the large truck that could have t-boned them was half a block away.

"Don't lose him," said Gertie.

"I'm not gonna ram him."

"I'm not asking you to ram him. I'm asking you not to

lose him."

"Shit."

The sirens were getting closer. Any moment now the trained professionals would take over the situation, and Charlene could go somewhere to throw up and tremble for a while.

The silver car ran another red light. Charlene followed.

Then the car pulled over to the side and slammed the brakes, tires squealing and smoke billowing into the air. The man got out of the car and hurried around to the passenger side.

"Slow down, slow down!" said Gertie. "He may be running from the sirens, not us. We're just a normal car."

Charlene applied the brakes, not quickly enough to make them squeal. Her hands were sweating so badly that she almost lost her grip on the steering wheel.

The man opened the passenger side door. He reached inside, scooped up the little boy, then ran off, leaving both doors open. He didn't look back at Charlene's car. As she pulled up behind his abandoned vehicle, he ran into an alley.

The sirens were really close. The cops would catch this guy for sure.

Without discussing it, Charlene and Gertie both opened their doors, got out of the car, and chased after him.

The man tripped and fell. The little boy cried out as his father landed on top of him. The man frantically got back up, grabbed his son's hand, and pulled him to his feet. He spun around and saw Charlene and Gertie standing in the alley entrance.

"He's my fucking son!" the man wailed at them.

Charlene took a step forward. "I know you love him.

Just let him go, okay? The cops are almost here. It's over."

The man reached behind his back.

It's gonna be a gun, it's gonna be a gun, it's gonna be a gun, thought Charlene.

It was indeed a gun. The man pulled his son close and pressed the gun against his head.

Charlene fought back a scream.

"I'll do it!" the man warned. "I'll kill both of us before I let anybody take him again!"

Charlene had absolutely no idea what to do. She was not a trained negotiator. She could completely mess this up if she said the wrong thing. She wanted to believe that the man was bluffing, that he'd never consider murdering his own son and then committing suicide, and that if she and Gertie just stood there the cops would quickly take over. But the man sure as hell didn't seem like he was bluffing. He looked legitimately ready to pull the trigger.

The boy was crying.

"You're scaring him," said Charlene. Had that been a stupid thing to say? She wasn't sure.

She glanced at Gertie, desperately hoping that Gertie wouldn't go for her gun. Gertie stood motionless, watching the man in horror. If she *was* planning to shoot him, she was doing an amazing job of not giving away her intention.

"This is fucked up," Charlene told the man. "No matter how bad things are in your life, and I can tell they're really bad, this is not the way to handle it. You get that, right?"

Was she being patronizing? She didn't want the man to feel like she was talking down to him. If he blew out his son's brains, would it be her fault? What the hell was she supposed to say to him?

"He's not going back to her," said the man. Tears began to stream down his face.

He was still talking. That was good. She just needed to keep him talking until the cops could get a sniper or something in place.

"I'm not going to pretend I have any say in that," Charlene told him. What a dumb thing to tell him. Of course she didn't have any say in it. Why would anybody believe that she did? "We were out here for something completely different. We're just bystanders who got involved. But I can tell you, watching from the outside, that this is fucked up. C'mon. Put the gun down. You don't have to let him go, but put the gun down."

"There's no way out," said the man. "The cops'll show up, they'll take my son, and I'll go to prison. You explain to me how that isn't the best-case scenario here!"

Should Charlene ask him his name? Isn't that what a professional negotiator would do? Try to form a personal connection?

Gertie was scratching her arm. Maybe she had an itch, or maybe she was planning to go for the gun. Charlene tilted her head toward Gertie and tried to shake it, just enough to send the almost-imperceptible message that she should *not* go for her gun.

Gertie lowered her hand. Either the itch was gone or she'd received the message.

Charlene returned her full attention to the man. He was absolutely right that prison was his best-case scenario here. To try to convince him otherwise would be a transparent lie. Unless...

"Let the boy go and run," said Charlene. "You can get away if you don't have him slowing you down."

The man let out an incredulous laugh. "I can't run away from the cops like that! They'll have helicopters and everything! My only hope was to drive out of town before they set up checkpoints, and that plan has turned to complete shit!"

"Fine. So the best-case scenario is you going to jail. That's still a better scenario than murdering your son and killing yourself."

"Better for who?"

"For you and your son! Jesus Christ, how can you not see that?" She hoped her tone didn't set him off.

The man said something, but he said it quietly and Charlene couldn't hear it over the sirens and his son's sobbing. Suddenly the sirens turned off and she could see the blue and red flashing lights reflecting off the brick walls of the alley.

"Tell them to stay away!" the man shouted. "I'll shoot him! If I see so much as a shadow of a cop, I'll pull the trigger!"

Gertie turned and waved her hands. "Stay back!" she called out. "Please, stay back!"

"I mean it! Don't think I won't do it!" Spittle flew from the man's mouth and he was pressing the gun so tightly against his son's head that it looked like he could accidentally break the boy's neck.

"He's serious!" Gertie shouted at the cops.

"Neither of you have to get hurt," Charlene said. "Let him go. Surrender to the cops. Don't give this a permanent bad ending."

He hadn't shot the boy yet. That meant he didn't want to shoot the boy. But if the cops didn't heed Gertie's warning, he might very well do it.

"She can't have him," the man said.

Charlene could hear commotion outside of the alley. She didn't know what procedure the authorities would use for this sort of thing, but she did very much believe the man when he said that he'd pull the trigger if he saw so much as a cop's shadow. Did the cops understand this? The bustle just out of her line of sight was really making her anxious.

"Can my friend talk to them?" Charlene asked the man. "Make it clear how serious you are?"

The man nodded. "She's not a hostage."

Charlene turned to Gertie. "Don't let them come in here."

Gertie hurried out of the alley.

"They're not going to try to take you by surprise," Charlene promised. "Now you should let your son go."

"No."

"What's his name?"

"None of your fucking business." There was snot pouring over his mouth, but he didn't have a free hand to wipe it away.

Maybe it was time to lie. "My father is a lawyer," Charlene said. "A fantastic one. If you let him go, and let the police take you away peacefully, I promise he'll get you the best deal possible, pro bono. He's good. He won't make this problem go away, but he'll make it better."

"Yeah?"

"Yeah."

For one very brief moment Charlene thought she'd actually talked the man out of his murder/suicide. But then he shook his head. "I've already gone through the courts. They took him away from me *before* this. I don't care if your dad is Atticus Finch. He's not going to fix

66

this."

Atticus Finch had lost the case he was known for, but this was not the time to point out the flaw in the man's literary reference.

Charlene wondered what the police were doing. Getting a sniper into place? Waiting impatiently for Charlene to talk him out of pulling the trigger? How the hell had she gotten herself into this? She was a restaurant server!

She had no idea what tactic to use next. Reverse psychology? Offer him a sexual favor? Just walk away and let the people who knew what they were doing resolve the situation? Try to disarm him herself?

Maybe that last idea wasn't so bad. Not in a "charge him and tackle him to the ground" way, of course, but if she moved slowly and carefully...

"May I walk over there?" she asked.

"Why?"

"Because I'd like to look into your eyes when we talk, and the cops are less likely to try to shoot you if I'm in front of you."

"Yeah, go ahead," he said. "But stop when I tell you to stop."

Charlene walked toward him, hands out to show they were empty and that she meant no harm. She had absolutely no intention of making any sudden moves, so in theory, the worst possible outcome for her personally would be a close-up view of a child getting shot in the head. That was a pretty damn bad outcome, but if she got closer maybe she could convince him to hand her the gun.

"That's close enough," he said when she was a few feet away.

She stopped.

"May I make a presumptuous statement?" she asked.

"I guess."

"The fact that you let me get this close means that you want a peaceful resolution to this. Why would you bother granting my request if you didn't think there was another way out? And now that we've established that you *don't* want to kill anybody, including yourself, why not lower the gun?"

"I'll never see him again."

"Let's pretend that's true, even though I don't believe that it is. Is that a reason to kill him? You still lose."

"And his mother loses too. I won't have her thinking she won. I won't have her laughing at me."

"Whatever issues you have with his mother, they're not his fault. He's your *son*, for God's sake! I can tell just by looking at him that he's a smart kid. Why extinguish that? Who knows what he could become? Who knows what he could do, what he could bring to the world? You're not just stealing from him, you're stealing from me."

Was this becoming too corny? She felt like she might be veering dangerously close to being cheesy, if she hadn't already crossed that line. She didn't want the man to say, "Oh, give me a break!" and start shooting.

"I don't want to kill him," the man said, sounding utterly broken. She wouldn't have been able to hear him if she hadn't walked closer.

"Good! Then fucking don't!"

His hand trembled a bit. That could mean that he was considering lowering the gun. It could also mean that he was preparing to pull the trigger.

"What's your name?" Charlene asked.

"Lee."

"Hi, Lee. How about you give me the gun? That would make my day so much better. We've already established that you don't want to do this, so why drag it out? Every second this goes on makes the resolution more difficult."

"If I let him go, will you trade places with him?"

"Excuse me?"

"I'll let him go if you'll be my hostage so I can get out of here."

Hell no, Charlene thought. *No way. Not a chance. I want the boy to survive but I'm not going to sacrifice myself for him. That's pure madness.*

"I can't do that," said Charlene, feeling like a selfish, cowardly monster.

"I won't hurt you. They'll just think I'm going to hurt you. I'll let you go after we get away."

"That...that really doesn't work for me."

The little boy looked at her, and though Charlene honestly didn't like kids very much, his expression was heartbreaking. How many psychologists was it going to take to fix this kid's brain after this was over? Society would be lucky if he wasn't snatching women off the street like the other psycho.

"All right," Lee said.

Charlene didn't know for sure that he meant, "*All right, then I guess I'll have to kill him now,*" but she suddenly decided that she couldn't take that risk. "Okay," she said. "I'll do it. I'll trade places with him. Shit."

"Come closer."

For a moment Charlene couldn't get her legs to work. Her legs were clearly smarter than her. But then she forced herself to walk up to Lee and the boy. She cursed her stupidity for getting into this mess. And, yeah, she cursed that bitch Gertie for dragging her into it. God, this was going to end horribly, wasn't it?

Lee looked past her. "Hey!" he shouted. "Hey! One of you cops! Show yourself!"

"*Let the boy go,*" said somebody over a megaphone. "*Nobody has to get hurt.*"

"Can you hear me?"

"*We can hear you.*"

"That's good enough, then! I just want it known for the record that this lady offered to trade places with my son! That was some pretty selfless shit and I want her to get credit for it!"

"*Understood.*"

Lee lowered the gun. He knelt down and kissed his son on the cheek. "Go," he said, giving him a gentle shove. "Go on. Go find Mommy."

The boy ran past Charlene.

"The hostage idea sounded good, but I don't think I'd get away with it. I don't want to live as a fugitive, and I wouldn't want you to get accidentally shot by a dumbass cop."

"I appreciate that."

Now that he had a free hand, Lee wiped his face. "You should step back," he said.

"What are you going to do?"

"I mean it. You should step back." He raised the gun again.

"No, please don't."

He smiled. "At least make sure your mouth isn't open."

The voice sounded over the megaphone. "*Don't do it!*"

Lee spun the barrel around, pointing it at his face, and pulled the trigger.

With a couple of extra seconds to prepare, he might have shoved the barrel of the gun into his mouth before he pulled the trigger, or placed it to his temple. But apparently he wanted to do the deed himself, before the police had a chance to take him out, because he shot himself from a few inches away. The bullet hit right beneath his eye, exiting the back of his head in a spray of red mist.

As blood streamed down Lee's face, Charlene just stood there, paralyzed.

The gun dropped out of Lee's hand. It struck the pavement but Charlene couldn't hear it over the ringing in her ears.

Lee dropped to his knees, then his body pitched forward.

Charlene was vaguely aware of frantic movement behind her, but she couldn't look away from the thin red rivulets that streamed away from his head.

Somebody put their arm around her, and she screamed and shook them off, even though she knew nobody was trying to kidnap her. She thought it might be Gertie, but, no, it was a female police officer. As more people rushed forward, Charlene doubled over, hacking but not actually vomiting, and violently swung her fists around so that nobody would touch her.

CHAPTER SIX

"Thank you! Oh, God, thank you!" a woman shouted at Charlene. She had an ugly bruise on the side of her face and her arms were tightly wrapped around the little boy.

Charlene ignored her.

A couple of minutes later, she sat in the back of an ambulance as a paramedic checked her out.

"I'm fine," she insisted. "He didn't do anything to me." Well, he might have permanently destroyed her hearing, and he definitely left some massive psychological damage, but there was nothing this paramedic could do for her.

"Just checking you out to be sure, ma'am," said the paramedic, shining a penlight into her eyes. When he was done with that part of the examination, Gertie was standing there.

"Congrats," she said.

"For what?"

"You saved the kid."

"The police would've saved him."

"We don't know that. The guy could be headed for the

state line right now."

"The guy blew his brains out. His dead body is about fifty feet away, if you want to check it out for yourself."

"I know what happened to him."

"He might not have done that if we hadn't interfered. I didn't know what the hell I was doing. If we'd just given the description of his car and left it at that, the police might've caught him without anybody dying."

"He did that to himself, Charlene. He threatened to kill his son and then he committed suicide. Surely you're not blaming yourself for that. You're not, right?"

"What I'm saying is that we don't know how it would've turned out if we hadn't chased him. He might have surrendered. They might have shot him in the leg."

"Yeah, and he might have done what he said he was gonna do—murder the kid and then turn the gun on himself!" Gertie looked completely flabbergasted. "We're the good guys here. If we hadn't been around, maybe the boy would never have gotten back with his mother. No, it didn't have a magical happy ending, but it could've been so much worse. What if we hadn't followed the car, and we heard later that the boy was found dead in a ditch? How would you feel?"

"I don't know how I'd feel. All I can say is how I feel now."

Gertie sighed. "Well, you were right there when it happened. You saw it and I didn't. Once the shock wears off and you can think about this rationally, you'll be proud of what you did. That little kid is back with his mother because of you. You'll realize that soon."

"I don't want to talk to you anymore," said Charlene.

"You mean now or forever?"

"I don't know."

"Are you going to talk to the press? I see a couple of news vans around. I'm sure they'll want to do an interview."

"Hell no."

Gertie nodded her understanding. "All right. I'll leave you alone since that's what you want, but if you change your mind about wanting to talk to me, call me, no matter what time, okay?"

Charlene waved her away. Gertie left.

"You're okay," said the paramedic. "Blood pressure's a little high, but that's obviously not a surprise. There's nothing we can do for your ears, but the ringing should stop soon, just like if you went to a really loud rock concert."

"Yeah. Great fuckin' concert."

"It's none of my business, but I'm with your friend on this one. I was here when the dad said you were willing to trade places. That asshole was already over the edge. How it worked out is how it worked out, but that's not on you."

The paramedic helped Charlene out of the ambulance. A heavyset police officer walked over to her. He didn't look like he agreed with Gertie or the paramedic's assessment of the situation.

He made her tell the whole story. Then he made her tell it again.

She told him the complete truth. They hadn't done anything criminal, just stupid, and of course he'd be questioning Gertie as well so any attempt to distort the truth ("We were simply out for a walk") would be discovered. The officer might chew her out, but she wouldn't be charged with manslaughter or anything like that, right?

"Anything else you think I should know?" the cop asked.

"Nope."

"All right. Some reporters want to shove microphones in your face. You can talk to them if you want, or we can get you past them and into your car."

"I'd love it if you got me past them."

"Will do."

"So am I in trouble?" Charlene asked.

"Do you think a jury would convict you?"

"I'd like to think not."

"You think correctly. You and your friend need to knock off this vigilante nonsense, but we've got one live child and one dead abductor. I'm sure a lot of people are perfectly happy with that result. Things play out a little differently, he shoots his son...well, public opinion might not be so rosy toward the person who took it upon herself to do a hostage negotiation. As it is, no, nobody is going to arrest you and say you're responsible for what that dipshit did to himself. I'm guessing there's a lot of praise headed your way. Enjoy the fame. It won't last, so don't squander it by beating yourself up. He's the one who pulled the trigger."

"Thanks."

"No problem. That's as much of a motivational speech as you're gonna get from me. Still want us to sneak you past the reporters?"

"Yes, please."

"Come with me."

Ken took out his cell phone. Almost one in the morning. Three missed calls from Vivian and about ten texts.

He shouldn't have stayed this long. But he didn't have to work tomorrow, and Vivian wouldn't bitch at him any less if he'd gotten home a couple of hours earlier.

Regina had been dead when he arrived. He hated that he missed the moment of her passing. He was often tempted to hasten the process, just so he'd get to watch them die, but that would be an act of mercy. The women wouldn't truly be starving to death. Why bother to give them a slow, agonizing, primal demise if he was going to prematurely end it?

Anyway, they were so weak by the end that it was difficult to tell when the moment of death actually happened. He'd been here when his third victim died, but he'd had to hold a mirror under her nose to be sure that she'd passed.

Olivia was still alive. Wasn't talking much anymore. Ken didn't mind. He didn't need for her to actually *do* anything while he watched. He was perfectly happy to sit there and watch her mostly motionless, beautiful body hang in the cage, her life very slowly seeping away, like an inflatable mattress with the tiniest pinprick of a hole in the side.

He stood up. "Would you like some more water before I go?" he asked. "I've got a bunch of yard work to do, so I won't be back tomorrow. I'd rather not come back and find you dehydrated."

Olivia nodded.

He brought over the stepladder, gave her some water, then carried the ladder and chair back to their place. He always carried them upon his departure and dragged them upon his arrival. There was no practical reason that he needed to move them to the far corner; obviously, nobody was going to disturb them while he was gone. He just liked the awful sound they made as they scraped across the concrete. It was a wonderfully unpleasant way to let his girls know that he was ready to watch them.

Ken took one last long whiff. He was a little ashamed of the way he enjoyed the room's smell. Death, vomit, piss...even a savage serial killer should find the aroma unpleasant. Not him. He'd bottle that scent and wear it as cologne if he could get away with it. Use it to season his food.

When he ran out of cages and had to empty the first one to make room for another victim, he'd probably hose down the floor as well. For now, everything that came out of the women stayed on the concrete.

He waved to Olivia, even though he was behind her and she couldn't see him. He waved to the corpses as well, enjoying the thought that their spirits might be forever trapped in their shriveled dead bodies and that they could see him waving to them. He opened the door and left the room.

Ken shut the door and entered the four-digit passcode to lock it.

He walked up the stairs and entered a different four-digit passcode to unlock the door at the top. He emerged into the main part of the house, shutting and locking the door behind him.

It was a small house in an isolated area. You could see

the neighbors off in the distance, but not hear them unless they were having a really loud party. Of course, the basement was completely soundproofed. As long as the door to the cage room and the door at the top of the stairs were both closed, a brand new healthy victim could be shrieking at the top of her lungs, and somebody standing where Ken was right now wouldn't hear a thing. Top-notch soundproofing. Not cheap.

The smell was easier to block. The basement was sealed up like a non-working freezer filled with rotting carcasses.

Of course, Ken couldn't afford to rent a second home like this on his own. It was a joint venture with his buddy Darrell. Ken handled all of the paperwork, making sure the rental couldn't be traced to either of them, and Darrell paid most of the rent. Ken got the basement. Darrell, who needed a place to screw his three mistresses, got the upstairs.

Ken said only that he needed the basement for "drug-related matters." Darrell never asked for more information. But Darrell *loved* to share his own tales of debauchery. He'd describe everything in graphic detail, and Ken would ask the appropriate questions with the appropriate leer on his face, even though it didn't much interest him that Darrell finally got Lydia to let him in the back door, or that Sarah liked her nipples twisted, hard.

They coordinated their schedules to make sure Darrell's side chicks didn't freak out because somebody else was in the house. Darrell's own schedule was further complicated by the fact that Lydia and Sarah knew about each other and were cool with it—though not cool enough to double up, damn it—but Jackie would not only lose her mind if she knew about Lydia and Sarah, but she'd freak if she found out that Darrell wasn't really divorced. "She'd tear my balls off and feed them to me," Darrell said with a chuckle.

Ken drove home, hoping Vivian would be asleep when he got there.

She wasn't.

"Where the hell have you been?" she asked.

"I love you too," he said, giving her a kiss. He made sure to give her a dose of his whiskey breath before their lips touched.

"I asked you a question."

"Am I not allowed to have friends? You have friends. Jared has friends. But not me, oh no, no friends for Kenneth! Why, he'd be shirking his grown-up responsibilities if he went out and enjoyed himself for once."

"I don't stay out all night with my friends."

"It's not all night. It's one-thirty. When did we become so old that we have to be in bed at a reasonable hour?"

Vivian ignored the hypothetical question. "And I call or text you to let you know where I am. How hard is it to send a text?"

"I have large thumbs."

"Don't be a smartass."

"Fine. I'm sorry I was out so very late. I had a few drinks and wanted to sober up before I drove home."

Vivian clenched and unclenched her fists. "Please stop lying to me. I know where you were and what you were doing."

"Is that so?"

"Are you going to tell me who she is, or should I wait to see her picture on the news?"

"I didn't kill anybody," said Ken, lowering his voice so

Jared wouldn't hear.

"Bullshit."

"I didn't kill anybody! I wasn't out on a hunt! I promised you that I'd tell you when I was going, and I'd never break that promise."

"You're out there too often. You're going to get caught."

Ken smacked his palm against his forehead in frustration. "What did I just say? Why aren't you listening to me? I didn't strangle anybody tonight." He held up his arms. "Do you see any new scratches? Any signs that somebody fought back? Anything? Want to check my fingernails for dirt? Do you want to check the shovel in the trunk? I swear to God, Vivian, I'm telling the truth. You know about all of them. Like you said, their pictures show up on the news."

"Maybe you've been killing outside of your type. How do I know you aren't murdering little girls?"

"Are you listening to yourself? Is your brain processing the words that are coming out of your mouth? I can't just go around strangling a new girl every other night. You don't think I'd get caught if I was digging that many graves? If I'm going on this massive slaughter spree, why isn't it on the news, huh? How come the news is only covering the ones you know about?"

"Maybe you're traveling."

"Yeah, that's it. That makes so much sense. How the hell would I get a little girl, anyway? You think I'm going to take the risk of talking to a strange child and have her run away and tell her parents?" He put his hands on Vivian's shoulders and looked into her eyes. "Vivian, honey, the eight women I've told you about are the only ones. I would never hunt without telling you. I know how bad things will be for you and Jared if I get caught, and I'd never put you through that."

"Then where were you tonight?"

"I was at a bar! I drink too much, okay? You married an alcoholic. I got drunk and I was irresponsible and inconsiderate. What do I have to do to convince you I wasn't out on a hunt? Just tell me and I'll do it!"

"Take me to the bar and let me verify your story with the bartender."

"The bar's closed. That's why I left. But we'll go tomorrow as soon as it opens, okay?" Ken knew that after a good night's sleep, Vivian wouldn't bother with this crap. But he'd have to start spending less time in the basement, at least until she had a week or so to chill out.

Vivian stepped away from him. "Are you hungry?"

"Yeah. I'll make something."

"Did this *bar* you were at have a television?"

"Three of them. Why?"

"Were any of those three televisions playing the news?"

"Just tell me what you're trying to say, Viv."

"I'm saying that the news was very interesting tonight."

Ken suddenly felt more than a little queasy. "Interesting how?"

"Don't crap your pants. The police aren't going to break down our door. Go make yourself some nachos or something, and I'll show you."

"Show me now."

He followed her to the dining room, where Vivian's laptop rested on the table. She sat down, clicked a few times, then turned the laptop so he could see.

"Tonight a Hornbeam Ridge man, Lee Montgomery, is

dead from a self-inflicted gunshot wound, following the abduction of his six-year-old son," said the newscaster, who wore too much makeup. "Montgomery set the boy free after a tense standoff, but took his own life before the authorities could arrest him. Two women saw Montgomery walking with his son and called 911 about his suspicious behavior. The women followed him until Montgomery ran from the vehicle and threatened to kill both his son and himself. One of the women, Charlene Fox, made efforts to talk Montgomery out of harming his son, going so far as to offer herself as a hostage instead."

The scene cut to a girl speaking to the camera. She wore a bad wig with straight brown hair. Ken leaned forward. The name "Gertie Richardson" appeared on the bottom of the screen.

"Yeah, we were terrified that he was going to kill his son," she said. "But my friend talked him down. She doesn't think she's a hero but I sure do. We were out there trying to save my cousin but she ended up saving somebody else instead. A completely crazy night."

The scene switched back to the newscaster and her male co-host. "Police say the young ladies were trying to serve as bait for whomever is responsible for as many as eight missing women over the past few months."

The other newscaster chuckled. "Sounds like he should be worried."

"The boy is back with his mother, who suffered moderate injuries at the hands of her husband. And now over to Stan with our Doppler weather radar report."

The news clip ended.

"Play it again," said Ken.

Vivian played the clip again.

"What does serving as bait even mean?" he asked.

"I guess it means that they were going to kick your ass."

"What do they think, that I'm careless? That I'm stupid? So, what, that bitch was just wandering around in a cheap wig waiting for me to leap out at her?"

"Wigs like that aren't cheap."

Ken wanted to tell his wife to shut up, but thought better of it. "I don't like that newscaster laughing at me. Who the hell does he think he is? Does he think I'm a joke? How hard would he be laughing if I killed his daughter?"

"If you go after the family of the news guy, you'll get caught for sure."

"I'm not really gonna do it. I'd love to, though. Make him do a live news report while he watches me choke her. Maybe I'll go after those two bitches. They want to be bait? I'll turn them into bait. Play it again."

Vivian shook her head and closed the laptop lid. "I didn't show you that so you could get all pissed off and vow revenge. I did it so you'd know to be careful. Maybe they're not the only ones trying to fool you. You swear that you're being careful when you choose your victims, but from now on you have to be even *more* careful. Maybe you should just stop for a while. Not forever, just for a while. A year or so."

"Maybe," said Ken.

He had no intention of stopping. He wasn't going to be stupid about it, but he wasn't going to let those girls think they were oh-so-brave and heroic. She thought she could end his reign of terror by walking around town in a wig? Seriously?

Ken wouldn't lose his cool. Wouldn't take any unnecessary risks. Wouldn't let the intense rage he was feeling work against him.

He wasn't going to promise himself that those bitches would end up in cages. But he would certainly investigate the possibility of making that happen.

CHAPTER SEVEN

Charlene groaned, rolled over, and looked at her alarm clock. 1:24. Her shift started in just over half an hour. She slapped her hand around on the nightstand until she located her cell phone, and called Travis.

"Hey," he said.

"I'm sorry, I can't come in today," she told him.

"I never thought you would. Take as long as you need. Until I hear differently, I'll assume that you're not coming in."

"Thanks." Charlene hung up. Her display showed that she had new voice mail messages from eleven different people. She'd give her mother a call so she could pass on a reassuring update. Everybody else could go to hell.

She was tempted to go back to sleep, but she'd had enough nightmares for a while, so she got out of bed. She took a really long, really hot shower. None of Lee's blood had gotten on her, and if any had it would've been washed off by last night's really long, really hot shower, but she vigorously scrubbed at her body anyway. She was tempted to just sit down in the corner and let the water cascade over her while she cried, but, no, that was too pathetic.

She got out of the shower, got dressed, and sat on the couch.

Spending the day watching television probably wouldn't improve her mental state.

Honestly, she couldn't think of any way to spend the day that wouldn't involve her reliving the moment where the bullet tore into Lee's face. She didn't feel any true sympathy for the guy—he had, after all, beat up his ex-wife and threatened to murder his son. The world was a better place without a piece of human garbage like him. It just wasn't easy to cope with the idea that a man had blown his brains out right in front of her and she might have been responsible for things happening that way.

If she was going to keep seeing the red mist, she might as well be earning money while she was doing it. She called Travis back.

"Changed my mind," she told him. "I'm coming in."

"You sure? We can work out something where I give you a couple of paid vacation days, if you want. Gertie is already trying to get the other servers to kick in some of their tips."

"No, I need to keep my mind off things. I'll be there in twenty minutes."

When she arrived, Travis was standing in the back room. "Don't go anywhere," he told her, as she punched in. Travis left, and then returned a minute later with all of the servers, chefs, bussers, and dishwashers following him. Travis stepped forward and addressed everybody.

"Everybody who works here is a hero. Each and every one of you. However, Charlene is a hero who rescued an abducted six-year-old, so let's show her some appreciation, okay?"

The entire restaurant staff applauded. There was also whistling. Gertie, beaming, applauded the most enthusiastically of all of them.

"Speech!" somebody said.

"No speech," Travis told him. "She's been through a serious trauma. Everybody be nice to her today. Okay, back to work."

Almost everybody left the back room. Charlene felt like she should be feeling bitchy about this display of appreciation that she'd never wanted, but it honestly made her feel pretty good.

Gertie walked over to her. "I know you need your space," she said. "Just checking to see how you're doing."

"I'm fine. They should be giving you credit, too."

"Oh, they did. They all lined up and applauded when I got here."

"Well, that was nice of them."

"Yeah." Gertie nervously scratched her neck. "So are we okay?"

"You mean as friends?"

Gertie nodded.

"I don't think so," Charlene told her.

"I never asked you to come with me. You volunteered."

"I completely, one hundred percent get that. I'm self-aware enough to know that I'm being irrational. And I may get over it. I'll let you know if I do."

"Okay. Thanks." Gertie looked like she wanted to say something else, but instead she turned and left the room.

Several of Charlene's customers recognized her. She got much larger tips than usual. Not one person gave her a disapproving wag of the finger and said, "Now, now, you ought to have minded your own business!"

It was entirely possible that everybody else was right. If she and Gertie had done nothing, the little boy could be halfway across the country right now trapped in a car with an emotionally disturbed woman-beater. If they'd done nothing, a police officer could be in mental anguish right now, beating himself up over accidentally shooting the boy when he was trying to take out the father. Maybe talking to Charlene instead of having a dozen cops point guns at him gave Lee the time to truly consider what he was doing, which is why he let his son go. In the alternate reality where they didn't follow him, he might have been surrounded, then panicked and immediately shot his son in the head.

Maybe.

Charlene wasn't ready to be at peace with this.

Gertie had worked an earlier shift and left without saying goodbye. After Charlene clocked out for the night, she considered sending Gertie a text just to reiterate that she was fine, but decided that she didn't feel like it.

She scrolled through her text messages. A few journalists wanting to interview her. (Three of them had come into the restaurant to speak with her, but Travis politely but firmly asked them to leave.) She'd already talked to her mother and asked her to pass along the message that she was okay, but she went through and sent quick responses to all of her relatives who'd texted. Then she did the same thing with her concerned friends. She ignored the journalists.

That left Megan.

She'd met Megan at a party a year ago. Slept with her a couple weeks after that. They'd had a few days of good times, then casually parted ways, happy to have met each other. If Megan was contacting her for a reprisal, well...that idea had a *lot* of appeal right now.

She texted Megan back: *Hi!*

The response came back immediately: *Hi, sexy!*

Yes, this was exactly how Charlene would get her mind off her problems.

When Charlene woke up the next day, all was right in the world. She stretched out happily in Megan's bed, pleased that several really intense orgasms had indeed been just the thing to bring joy back to her life. Perhaps Megan was simply being a star-fucker, but that was totally fine. Her immensely talented fingers earned her the right to bask in Charlene's momentary celebrity.

Megan rolled over, yawned, and smiled. "Good morning, sexy."

"It's afternoon."

"Is it?" Megan glanced over at the clock, which read 12:52. "Damn. Guess we were up late."

"Very late. It's like we were too preoccupied with something to go to sleep at a normal hour."

"We just let the time get away from us. I suppose we should get out of bed and put on clothes so we can leave the apartment and have a nice productive day."

"You're absolutely right," said Charlene. "However, I would also like to suggest an alternative course of action, one where we don't get out of bed, and we don't get dressed. I haven't figured out all of the details yet, but I honestly think we could make this plan work."

"I'm willing to give it a shot," said Megan, climbing on top of her.

Charlene was still feeling good as she arrived at work. She and Megan had not discussed what happened in the alley, and Megan hadn't pushed for any details after Charlene said she didn't want to talk about it. They hadn't made any plans to meet later, and maybe they wouldn't see each other until the next time she did an impromptu hostage negotiation. Either way, she wasn't necessarily *cured* (and, in fact, her ears were still ringing from the gunshot, though not nearly as badly as they were Friday night) but she was infinitely better.

"You look like you had a good night," said Gertie, as Charlene put on the black apron all of the servers wore.

"What makes you say that?"

"Those are the same clothes you wore yesterday."

"Maybe I sat on the couch all night in a depressed funk and couldn't bring myself to change my clothes."

Gertie's face fell. "Oh, shit, I'm sorry. You just looked so cheerful that I—"

"I'm kidding. I got super-laid last night. The details are so hot that I honestly believe I could turn you into a raging dyke if I shared them, so I'm keeping them to myself to protect your heterosexuality."

"I'm not trying to protect it. I mean, it would open more options."

"Sorry. A lady doesn't eat pussy and tell." She froze. "Travis heard that, didn't he?"

"No, he's nowhere around."

"Okay, good. I thought I felt him staring at me. Anyway, does it go without saying that I'm never going to join you on another one of your expeditions?"

"Very much so. Also, they're over. I didn't tell any news people why we were out there, but I guess it was part of the public report, and they blabbed it on TV. Even in the unbelievably unlikely event that I happened to be walking where he was seeking his prey, my plan's been spoiled. He'd either leave me alone or he'd just shoot me. So there's nothing I can do to help find Kimberly except wait for somebody else to do it."

"I'm sorry."

"Don't worry about it. Like we've already established, it was really more of a selfish thing to make me feel like I was doing some good. It would've felt great to slam my stun gun into his balls, but it wasn't ever going to happen. I just got tired of putting up 'Missing' signs. Anyway, I'm glad you got laid. I should get back to work before Travis yells at me."

"Hold up," said Charlene. "I'm still pretty messed up in the head over what happened, but I'm not cursing your existence or anything like that."

"Thank you. That means a lot."

"Also, you looked ridiculous in that wig."

Gertie laughed. "I agree."

"Okay, now you can get back to work."

93

Ken's day at work was driving him absolutely batshit insane. That was par for the course, but today was even worse, because he couldn't get those women from the news out of his mind.

How dare they? It would be different if they were cops. He didn't mind that, even the female ones—they were just doing their jobs.

But he didn't care if it *was* her (long-dead) cousin. It infuriated him that they thought they could trap him like that. What were those tiny girls going to do to him? Overpower him? Shoot him? If they shot him, they'd never find her cousin's body—he was good at covering his tracks, which is why Darrell trusted him to rent the house for them.

He didn't even care if he got to put them in cages. A strangulation, like the kind Vivian thought he did, would be fine. Squeeze their necks until their eyeballs popped out. Maybe he'd slash their throats. Maybe he'd get into Darrell's stash of S&M gear and whip their backs until they were a mess of blood.

Damn, he was so angry that his hands were trembling. Made it difficult to work on this spreadsheet.

He hated this job. A waste of forty hours a week, not counting the commute and his unpaid lunch break. Without this job, he could be spending all day every weekday in the basement. He'd used a couple of vacation days for that purpose, but he obviously couldn't quit. Vivian would notice if he stopped getting paychecks, and though she didn't track his vacation time, she'd question if he came up short when they wanted to actually go somewhere.

So he was stuck here, staring at these numbers all day.

He wondered what those girls were doing right now.

Laughing at him?

High-fiving each other for their amazing victory in getting the dad to shoot himself in the face?

Getting bombarded with lucrative offers for the movie and book rights to their story?

The rights to their story would be far more valuable after their bodies were discovered, though of course they wouldn't be able to enjoy the money themselves.

He wouldn't go after them right away. Unless they were complete idiots, they'd be on high alert. He'd give their lives a chance to calm down before he entered it.

But if they wanted to meet him, he was happy to oblige. On his terms.

Olivia tried to refuse water.

Her existence was hell on earth and she wanted it to end. She thought she'd read that you could live for several weeks without food, but she'd be dead much sooner if she didn't drink any of the water he offered.

She tried. She really tried.

But she was so thirsty, so, *so* thirsty, that when he climbed up to her cage with the bottle and the straw, she frantically drank. And for a few moments she felt better. Then she once again became aware of the unbearable hunger.

She fantasized about him getting bored with her, grabbing her dry, lifeless hair and yanking her head back until her neck snapped. Suffering over. Paradise.

He didn't. He just watched her.

CHAPTER EIGHT

Charlene was surprised by how quickly things returned to normal. It wasn't all happy thoughts, all the time—it was still ridiculously easy for her to conjure up the mental image of Lee killing himself, and it didn't help that she had to serve a lot of dishes with red sauce. (She was able to keep this observation to herself. Travis might not fire her for dumping food on a customer, but he probably couldn't employ servers who compared their food to splattered brain matter.) And she had terrible dreams every night, although they faded from her memory seconds after she woke up, leaving her with the knowledge that she'd had a horrific nightmare but no details. But she was able to live her life pretty much the way she'd done it before.

By the third day, the ringing in her ears was gone. Reporters had stopped contacting her well before that. The twenty-four hour news cycle had moved on and she was no longer of any interest. Gertie had been interviewed on local and cable news in the aftermath, but it didn't lead to anything but a few minutes of airtime. She was still a restaurant server. Customers didn't recognize her anymore. Though the police had said they might need to follow up, it was a week later and they hadn't tried to get in touch, and Charlene assumed that they wouldn't require any more of her insight.

She and Gertie were cordial to each other, and not in a phony, overly formal way. They even joked around a bit, though never about the actual incident. But they didn't hang out after work, and if Gertie did make that offer, Charlene would decline. She wasn't sure yet if she'd fabricate an obviously fake excuse or just tell Gertie point-blank that she wasn't interested.

She got together with Megan once more, and then they mutually stopped contacting each other. Charlene was okay with a completely superficial, "only about the sex" encounter every once in a very long while, but for the most part it wasn't her thing. She liked Megan well enough, but she'd never date her, and she knew Megan felt the same way, so they settled for a couple of orgasm-packed nights and then cheerfully went their separate ways again.

Tonight her plans were to stay home and read. She ordered a pizza and checked her e-mail. Only one message stood out amongst the spam:

Hi, Charlene! Warren Taywood here. I wanted to wait for things to calm down for you before I got in touch. I'm starting a new web series called "Deep Dive Into Heroism," where we do an hour-long look at people like you who risked their own lives to save others. Very uplifting and inspiring stuff, but not sappy. We're a small startup venture, but there would be some pay involved, and you'd get to tell your story in more than a sound bite. I'd love to meet for dinner (my treat!) and I can give you an overview of my vision for the project. If you're interested, let me know your availability and we'll set something up. Thanks! – Warren.

She considered just ignoring it, but decided to write back.

Thanks for thinking of me. I'm not really interested in talking about my experience, so I'll have to pass. Sorry.

Before the pizza arrived, he'd responded.

I understand. However, I think you'll like the approach I'm going to take with the material. It won't be exploitative or sensationalized. It'll be a very respectful project, focusing on you as a person and not dwelling on any of the gory details. I'd also let you see the episode before it went live, and if you REALLY weren't comfortable with it I simply wouldn't upload it. (I can make that promise because I'm sure you'd be happy with it.) If nothing else, you can get a free meal out of giving me the opportunity to describe the project in person. You pick the restaurant. Appetizers and dessert included. Please consider it. – Warren.

Charlene wrote back immediately.

No.

She closed the lid of her laptop. The pizza arrived a few minutes later, and she settled in for a night of pepperoni, extra cheese, and erotica.

Thanks, Warren, typed Gertie. *I'd be interested in discussing this further. I work until 10:00 PM for the next three nights, so a lunch meeting would work better. As long as I'm done by around 1:30 PM I can get together anytime this week.*

Ken frowned at the computer screen. What the hell

was Charlene Fox's problem? Uptight bitch. He could solve that problem with money. If he told her that his investors had authorized a payment of, say, five thousand dollars, she'd at least meet with him. He had to wait, though. Didn't want to seem too desperate and make her think he had an ulterior motive. He sent back a polite e-mail thanking her and asking her to let him know if she changed her mind. He'd follow up later. He was in no hurry.

The other girl was also a problem. He didn't want to meet her for lunch. He wanted their conversation to end after dark. In a perfect world, he wouldn't meet her at a restaurant at all, but he couldn't imagine that she'd show up at a private location to speak with him. If she was *that* dumb, he probably wouldn't even kill her, knowing that her own day-to-day existence was enough of a struggle.

Actually, he wrote back, *I've got a lot going on this week and it might be better to wait until Thursday anyway. Can you do 6:00?*

He glanced at what he'd written. That didn't sound desperate, did it? Would she question his motive? If she pushed back, he'd go with a lunch meeting, which he'd use to put her at ease so he could set up another meeting for a future and more dangerous time.

He sent the e-mail.

Stared at his screen until she replied.

That works!

You pick the place, he typed. *I'll be there at 6:00.*

Red Lobster?

See you there!

For the next three days, Ken paid only quick visits to the basement after work. It helped keep Vivian off his ass and made his home life a little more bearable. He even wished he could do it on an extended lunch break, but Darrell had daytime dibs on the house Monday through Friday unless Ken specifically made plans ahead of time. Ken had shown up once, only a couple of weeks after they started renting the house, and Darrell had coerced him into videotaping the encounter, using an actual VHS recorder to ensure that nothing could accidentally get uploaded to the internet. It had not been a pretty sight. It wasn't anything Ken wanted to see in the first place, but they'd mostly stuck with missionary, which meant that his primary visual was Darrell's enormous gyrating ass. After that, he made it a point to respect their schedules.

So he went after work, staying only long enough to water Olivia and watch her for a few minutes.

She'd succumbed to madness by now, and it was a glorious thing to witness. He could tell there was a movie playing in her mind, and it wasn't a happy musical. When she spoke, she made no sense. Sometimes it was a string of random words, and sometimes it was pure gibberish. If he'd recorded it and played it for somebody, they'd be so creeped out they wouldn't sleep for days.

With all of his victims, he wondered what they'd do if he let them out of the cage. Not much, obviously, but would they just lie there? Would they try to make their arms and legs work in a feeble, clearly doomed effort to drag themselves to the door?

It would be compelling to watch. A beautiful sight. But it was a pain to get them into the cages, and having them desperately flail around on the filthy basement floor wasn't part of his overall plan. They could get hurt. If they got hurt, they could die sooner. He didn't want that.

Researchers would probably be fascinated by what he was doing. There really weren't many opportunities to study a healthy, well-fed person as they suffered through a complete lack of any nourishment whatsoever. It would be very difficult for a scientist to observe this process without giving the person a sandwich every once in a while. Really, he should be writing down detailed notes and taking daily pictures of their failure to thrive. Make a photographic diary as their bodies devoured themselves from the inside.

But...no. This was for him and him alone.

Ken made a halfhearted attempt to initiate sex that Vivian rejected. That didn't bother him. He was in the mood for a blowjob, but Vivian would want reciprocation, and he was *not* in the mood for that. They just sat up in bed, watching television.

"I've got a date tomorrow," he said.

"What?"

"Remember those girls who tried to catch me? The ones who got that guy to shoot himself?"

Vivian spent a few seconds trying to find the remote control. She picked it up and muted the television. "Of course I remember them. What do you mean, you have a date?"

"One of them thinks I'm interested in doing a TV show about her. We're meeting for dinner tomorrow. So I'll be home late."

"Are you out of your mind?"

"Why doesn't it surprise me that you're about to overreact?"

"Overreact?" asked Vivian. "You just told me that you're going to meet a girl for dinner and then strangle her and you think I'm overreacting?"

"I never said I was going to strangle her."

"Oh, gosh, I'm so sorry. My mistake. So you've become a television producer now, huh?"

"I told her it was a web series. I think that's more believable. I'm going to gain her trust. If things work out and I can do it safely, yeah, she gets to be Victim #9. But more likely than not I'm just setting the stage for getting her in the future. Building her trust. She won't go anywhere with me tomorrow, but if I can convince her that I'm legitimate and we set up a place for filming, maybe she'll drop her guard and show up."

"What happened to the whole idea of random victims only?"

"That's still my overall plan. I think this is worth making an exception, don't you?"

Vivian just gaped at him. "No. I absolutely do not. She's exactly the kind of person where you *don't* make an exception. The police know she was trying to lure you into attacking her. If she disappears, they'll know who did it."

Ken shook his head. "No, they'll know that the mystery man kidnapping women did it. They won't know it's me."

"It adds a connection to you. She'd tell people about you. You didn't have multiple encounters with any of the others. This is getting too close."

"Have a little faith in me, Viv. I'm not telling her my

real name. I'll be wearing a disguise."

"Do you really think witnesses couldn't identify you just because you had a fake beard?"

"It's a gigantic fake beard. With that and the glasses, no, people who would have no reason to try to remember my face won't recognize me." He also liked to wear a conspicuous bandage. If somebody said that he had a bandage on his neck, but had no wound there if he was questioned out of disguise, it was one more detail to throw them off the track. "I'm not going to take any chances. If we meet more than once and I think the second time is too risky, I'll drop the whole idea. She gets to live."

"So it's just one of them?"

"Yeah. The one who wore the wig. The other one said no."

"Where are you meeting her?"

"Red Lobster."

"Did she pick it?"

"Yeah."

"So she could be a regular there?"

Ken hesitated. "Maybe."

"So people could recognize her? Maybe a favorite waiter? People who could say, 'Oh, I wonder who she's with?' Those kinds of people?"

"I wanted her to choose the place so she'd feel more comfortable. She'd have no reason to be suspicious. I wanted her to know that we'd be in a safe, public spot."

"Well, that's good for her, but that could blow up in your face. I don't care if your fake beard covers your entire face, you don't have dinner with a victim where people might know her. That's just idiotic. How did you get in touch with her?"

"E-mail?"

"A secure address?"

"Of course."

"Are you sure?"

"No, honey, I created a Gmail account that any teenage hacker could trace back to me. Jesus. I know how to keep my messages private."

"I'm sure you do."

Ken glared at her. "What's that supposed to mean?"

"Are you going to try to have sex with her after your little date?"

"Is that supposed to be a joke?"

"Did it make you laugh?"

"No, I'm not going to try to have sex with her. Nor did I try to have sex with any of the others. I can't believe you'd even say that to me. Is that why you're so upset? Because you think I'm cheating on you?"

"I'm upset because you're taking a suicidal risk. You're going to get caught. You swore to me that they'd all be random victims. You're still getting your little 'long dark hair' fetish in there—"

"That's coincidence."

"—but they'd all be strangers. No friends. No co-workers. No casual acquaintances."

"She's not any of those things."

"She becomes a casual acquaintance when you have dinner together at her favorite restaurant and then make plans to meet again in the future. It's too dangerous. Do you think I want to be known as the wife of a serial killer? What do you think that will do to my life? Jared's life? Can you imagine the hell we'll go through if you get caught? Are you giving any consideration to your family?"

"I wouldn't tell anybody that you knew."

"Well, no, you probably wouldn't have the chance, because you'd go down in a hail of police gunfire. I'd like to think that while you lay on the sidewalk choking on your own blood your final words wouldn't be to rat me out."

"Okay, you know what, I feel like this has stopped being a reasonable conversation."

"I'm not worried about going to prison as your accomplice. I'm worried about having the man I married be exposed as a psychopath who strangles women."

"You think I'm a psychopath?"

"Are you under the impression that people *won't* call you a psychopath?"

"I'm asking what you think."

"Ken, we've been through this. Don't go getting your fragile feelings hurt. You know what point I'm trying to make. I know what it takes to bring you peace inside, and I support you, but this is outside of the bounds of our agreement."

Ken was silent for a moment. "I understand what you're saying. I do. It makes perfect sense. But it really, truly upset me to see those girls on the news. I can't get it out of my mind. It keeps me up at night. I can't focus at work. I have to do something about it."

Vivian put her hand on his leg. "Then be smarter about it. We'll meet in the middle. You have to take her someplace where people don't know her. If that means she gets too suspicious to meet you, then you'll just have to suck it up. But you're not asking her to come out to a cabin in the woods with you. It's a restaurant. Pick one neither of you have been to before. If she's on such high alert that she won't go to a new restaurant, then it's too dangerous for you to meet her."

"What do I tell her?"

"You tell her, hey, how about this other restaurant instead? Again, if it's a huge red flag for her, then it should be a huge red flag for you. You pick a place where neither of you will be recognized and you get a booth in the back. You make her feel comfortable. If she doesn't want alcohol, you buy whatever fancy non-alcoholic drinks they have, and keep ordering them for yourself and encouraging her to have them as well. At some point she'll get up to pee. Drug her drink. Get her to the car. Drive her someplace secluded and do the deed. Bury the body."

"All right."

"But if you *can't* get a booth in the back where nobody is watching you, and if she *doesn't* get up to go to the bathroom, or if she gives any indication that she doesn't believe you're some YouTube content provider, you ditch the whole idea. I mean it. *Any* indication. If she raises an eyebrow and you can't specifically identify why that eyebrow went up, you abort the mission. If you get the faintest tingling of your Spidey-sense, it's done. She goes free. Does that sound fair?"

Ken had to admit that it did. "Yes," he said. "It sounds completely fair."

"I still think it's a bad idea, but if you promise to stick to that plan, I won't stand in your way."

"I won't veer from the plan at all. It's a brilliant plan." He gave her a quick kiss on the lips. "I wouldn't do anything to put our family in jeopardy. I care about you and Jared too much."

"I'm trusting you."

"I won't betray that trust. And I wasn't going to try to

have sex with her. I'm not even going to flirt with her. She'll know me as a web series producer, and then her executioner. That's it."

"I'm glad," said Vivian.

They kissed.

CHAPTER NINE

*H*i, *Gertie! It turns out that one of my investors will be in town on Thursday, so I've got a meeting with her that'll keep me from making it to Red Lobster by six. I'm not sure where you're located, but what if we switched to the Shellfish Grotto? That's near Hornbeam Ridge, so I know you've driven out that way before. ☺ Not that I'm a snob, but it's much better seafood and it's not a chain. If that doesn't work for you, we can figure something else out. Sorry for the inconvenience! —Warren*

I hadn't heard of The Shellfish Grotto, but I just read some online reviews and it sounds fantastic. A lot more expensive than Red Lobster, though. Are you sure? We can always just push our meeting back to later in the evening. I have nowhere else to be.

Hi, Gertie! Thank you for thinking about my pocketbook. (Do people say "pocketbook" anymore? Do you even know what that

is? LOL.) Though I'd like to pretend that I'm such a sweetheart that I'm paying for this fine expensive meal out of my own bank account, it's actually counted in the production costs of the show, so my investors are picking up the tab! I should've suggested it in the first place. —Warren

Sounds great, then. Looking forward to it!

Ken waved to Gertie as the server led her to his booth. He'd arrived at the restaurant half an hour early to increase his chances of getting a table in the back, without Gertie knowing that he'd specifically requested one. He agreed with Vivian that there could be absolutely no suspicion on Gertie's part if he was going to get away with this, so he wasn't taking any chances. And if he had to abandon the plan...well, he'd probably do it. His criteria for when it was time to let her escape might not be as stringent as Vivian's, but he wasn't going to be careless about it.

She was wearing a fancy dress and make-up, like she was out on a date or wanted to look like she was ready for the cameras. She was actually pretty damn hot when she wasn't wearing that stupid wig.

Ken stood up to greet her. "Hi, I'm Warren," he said, shaking her hand. "Great to meet you."

"Great to meet you, too. I'm Gertie, obviously."

They slid into opposite sides of the booth. Ken

gestured to the drink menu that was on her side. "Order whatever you want."

"Thanks." Gertie glanced up at the server. "Think I'm just going to have a Diet Coke."

The server nodded and left.

"Keeping my budget reasonable already," said Ken. "Did you have any trouble finding the place?"

"Nope. The GPS took me right here. Found a parking spot, no problem. Off to a promising start." Gertie opened the menu. "What's good here?"

"The crab cakes as an appetizer. For your main course, you really can't go wrong with any of their fresh catch fish. I've heard the fried shrimp is good but I've never had it."

"Maybe I'll do the salmon."

"Excellent choice."

"What are you getting?"

"The salmon was my pick, too."

"Oh, good." She closed the menu. "That was easy."

"So do you want to hear about *Deep Dive Into Heroism*?"

"Of course."

"Each episode is an hour. I know that sounds long for a web series, but we may try to shop it to the larger streaming services after we've got a few episodes under our belt. It's mostly going to be interviews with, well, heroes. Like you and your friend. I wish she was here."

"Yeah," said Gertie. "She's not really into any of this. She's way more of a quote unquote hero than I am. I was the driving force, but she's the one who saved the kid. Of course, she's also the one who saw the father...well, you know the story. If I'd seen that, I might not be here with you, either."

"I understand. Anyway, the interview will be a

straightforward setup. You in a chair against a green screen. One camera that you look into and one camera on the side. We'll make sure to get whatever you think is your best side." Ken chuckled. "We'll intercut it with other shots, but there aren't going to be any cheesy re-enactments or any of that nonsense. We'll get footage of the alley where it happened, and shots of the streets where you were walking around at night—that kind of stuff."

"You said it wouldn't be sensationalized, right? No shots of blood on the ground in the alley?"

"Oh, no, nothing like that. That's a whole different kind of documentary. Really, this is about you. Your motives. What you were thinking. How you worked up the courage to do what you did. And how it's affected you in the immediate aftermath."

"It sounds good."

"I want to save most of my questions for the show so that it's all fresh and unrehearsed, but I do want to get some basic insight first. Do you—"

The server arrived with Gertie's drink and then took their orders.

"I forget what I was going to ask," said Ken.

"Something that started with 'Do you.'"

"It'll come to me. In the meantime, what questions do you have for me?"

"When would we do this?"

"Whenever you can come back to my studio. Now, the interview will take quite a bit longer than what we use on the show. It'll be at least a couple of hours, maybe three or four, and we'll cut it down."

"So you'll get rid of the parts where I babble and stumble over my words and start picking my nose because I forget that I'm on camera?"

"Yes, indeed. We'll make you look good, I promise. What I'd love to do, if you're available, is get you over there tonight so you can meet the rest of the crew and do some camera tests. They're all in the studio working on one of our other projects."

"I can't do it tonight, but I can do it pretty much any other day. Whatever works for you. If I've got a day or two notice I can swap shifts with one of the other servers."

"Fair enough," said Ken. It had been too much to hope that she'd willingly go back to his "studio" tonight.

"And it's okay if I bring a friend, right?"

"Charlene?"

"No, just somebody to come along with me. They'll stay out of the way."

"I swear to God we're not making a porno."

"I know, I know."

"That is totally fine. We want everybody to feel safe and comfortable. Don't bring your whole entourage, but, yes, if you want to bring a friend, that is absolutely not a problem. We'll put him to work!"

"Thanks," said Gertie. "I'm not saying that I don't trust you. But of course this whole thing happened because women were disappearing!"

"Yep. There is no way I can argue that point. I should've been the one to suggest it, honestly. Pay will be a thousand bucks, flat fee. It's not a lot, but it works out to a pretty good hourly wage."

"Oh, no, that's great. I work for tips, basically. I wasn't even going to try to negotiate."

"So do you think you might be interested?"

"Definitely."

"That's great," said Ken. "I'm thrilled to hear it. And our food hasn't even arrived yet. I guess we could have discussed this over coffee."

"I guess we'll just have to suck it up and enjoy a nice meal."

"Sounds like an evening well spent."

Warren didn't seem like he was trying to hit on her. Gertie figured he would've taken off his wedding ring if that were the case. Of course, it always left an imprint or a tan line and the guys weren't fooling anybody, but that didn't stop them from trying.

She sure as hell didn't feel comfortable enough to go back to his studio tonight. She was reasonably confident that everything would be fine, and if she got a bad feeling about it she'd simply refuse to go inside, and if he pressured her she'd zap the shit out of him with the stun gun in her purse. But though she didn't get a bad vibe from Warren, going to a non-public place with him after dinner simply wasn't an option. Not for a web series shoot, not for sex, not for anything.

This wouldn't go in a romantic direction even if he were single. A lot of it was superficial stuff, but he was at least ten years older than her and kind of chubby. Though he pulled off the hipster beard thing pretty well, she wasn't a big fan of facial hair. It wasn't a deal-breaker by any means, but it did typically make her less inclined to imagine that there'd be kissing afterward.

In less superficial territory, his personality was...fine. He was friendly and pleasant to talk to and clearly had multiple functioning brain cells. There just wasn't any strong connection. She preferred guys with a sharper wit. A heartier laugh—he laughed, but it didn't quite reach his eyes.

Not that any of this mattered. He'd made no indication that he was trying to get into her pants, or that his interest in her was any different from their stated reason for having dinner together.

She really wished Charlene would be part of what Gertie jokingly called "the publicity tour" but which was really limited to a few quick interviews. It wasn't as if she was shamelessly cashing in on the situation—this would be the first paid interview, and nobody had yet offered to make a major motion picture out of her life story—yet she couldn't help but feel a little bit guilty about getting all of this praise while Kimberly was still missing. Gertie knew that Kimberly was almost certainly dead, and she wasn't sure if that made the publicity tour better or worse. If Charlene was along for the ride with her, she'd feel better about the whole experience.

Her parents, and even her aunt, had assured her that she was doing nothing wrong. (Though, not surprisingly, they emphatically did not approve of her trying to offer herself up as bait for the abductor.) It wasn't as if she was embarking on a vile cash grab like selling authorized t-shirts or charging for pictures. She made sure to give Charlene the appropriate credit every time she spoke to the media. She truly believed that they'd done a good deed, even if the piece of shit father killed himself, and she didn't see anything wrong with talking about it.

The salmon was delicious. Warren suggested pairing it with a glass of white wine, but she stuck with Diet Coke. As they ate, he asked a lot of questions but didn't seem all that interested in the answers. He didn't check his cell phone or stare at other women or anything like that, but there was very much a "just waiting for his turn to talk" facet to the conversation. Warren wasn't a very good storyteller, offering up anecdotes about his childhood in Michigan that ended without much of a point, and it was entirely possible that she was subconsciously doing the "waiting for her turn to talk" thing as well.

When the server offered dessert, she felt guilty about saying yes, but this wasn't a date. She was still going to do his show, and he wasn't paying for the meal himself, so why not indulge in the seven-layer chocolate cake?

"Do you want to split it?" she asked.

"Sure."

"One cake, two forks," said the server. "Got it."

As the server walked away, Gertie pushed back her chair. "I shouldn't have had that third Coke. Back in a minute." She picked up her purse and headed to the restroom.

Ken wasn't sure if she didn't trust him to be alone with her purse, or if she was on the rag. Either way, half of her drink was left. Rich chocolate cake tended to make you thirsty. She might finish it off.

He glanced around. There were other diners, but none of them were at adjacent tables, and none of them were looking at him. The restaurant had a nice dim atmosphere. He could empty the tiny vial into her drink in two seconds. Everybody seemed immersed in their meals and conversations.

He took the vial out of his pocket. Keeping it hidden under the table, he twisted off the lid.

A busboy walked over to the booth in front of theirs and began to pick up dishes and put them in his plastic tub.

Damn it.

The busboy wasn't looking at him.

If he asked Vivian what she thought he should do, she would lose her shit over the idea of him even considering trying to drug Gertie's drink when somebody was standing right there. But Vivian had no emotional investment in Gertie's fate. She didn't care what happened. It would destroy Ken to have wasted an evening in this stupid restaurant when he could've been sitting in the basement.

If the busboy happened to glance over, Ken was utterly screwed. There was no alternate explanation except that he was trying to slip drugs into Gertie's drink.

It was too risky.

If he got caught, he'd spend the rest of his life in prison, cursing the moment of sheer stupidity when he broke the very smart rule that he and Vivian had set.

Let her go.

Nobody was watching him.

He quickly poured the contents of the vial into his mouth.

Nobody noticed.

He reached across the table, picked up Gertie's glass, and pretended to take a drink while letting the clear liquid run out of his mouth into her Diet Coke. He set the glass back.

Nobody noticed that, either. If they had, they'd just have thought he was taking a drink of her soda. No big deal. Maybe they were married and didn't have beverage boundaries.

He picked up his glass of water, took a drink, swished it around, and spat it back. Then did it once more.

Success!

It's going fine, Gertie texted as she sat on the toilet. *About to have dessert. He's not a weirdo or anything.*

Thanks for the update, Charlene texted back. *You're going straight home after dinner?*

Yes. I'll let you know when I've left. Nothing to worry about, though. I don't think you'd like him but he's not sleazy.

What's for dessert?

Chocolate cake!!!

Enjoy!

"Here you go," said the server. Ken wasn't a big fan of chocolate cake, but it sure looked fancy. "All on one check?"

"Yes, please. As soon as you're ready."

"I'll go get it now."

Gertie returned to the booth just as the server left. "Oh my God, that looks good."

"Dig in."

Gertie picked up her knife and divided the cake into two equal sections. Apparently she didn't want to catch his germs. *Well, fuck you, too.*

After they'd had a couple of bites, the server returned with the check. Seventy-one bucks and they hadn't even ordered alcohol. More reason to be pissed if Gertie escaped. He took out his wallet, counted out four twenties and a five, which was neither a memorably good tip nor a memorably bad one. Right in line with what society said he was supposed to give her. "No change," he told the server as she collected the cash.

He occasionally wished he had a credit card under a fake name, but he didn't have the resources to make that happen, so it was always cash payments in situations like these. Though most diners paid with credit cards, leaving eighty-five bucks in cash wasn't weird enough to call attention to him.

He and Gertie continued to eat the cake. She raved about its sheer deliciousness, while he found it sickeningly sweet. He pretended that it was simply delectable, of course.

She wasn't drinking any of her Diet Coke.

He wasn't sure how to encourage her to take a drink. It would be strange to suggest to another adult that they finish their beverage. He could take a drink of his water to send a subtle reminder that her drink existed, but it had trace amounts of Rohypnol in it, so that would be a remarkably poor choice on his part.

They finished the cake. She scraped up the frosting from her side of the plate, getting every last trace.

How did you convince somebody to take a drink without it seeming unusual?

"That was some seriously good cake," he said. "Made me thirsty."

God, that was lame. Why had he said that? He picked up his glass and pretended to take a drink, not letting any get into his mouth. He set down the glass.

Gertie didn't take a drink from hers.

Goddamn it.

There was nothing he could do. Unless she grabbed it and took one last swig as they got up to leave, she was going to leave the glass half-full.

"Should we head off?" she asked.

No, he wanted to say. *How about you finish that fucking glass of Diet Coke that I paid for, bitch?*

"Yep," he said, sliding out of the booth.

Gertie slid out of the booth as well. She did not pick up the glass for one last swig.

They walked together toward the restaurant exit.

Gertie wanted to throw up.

She wouldn't have drank from a glass that she left unattended anyway. And the fact that his eyes kept darting to her glass didn't *necessarily* mean that he'd done anything to it. He'd have to be incredibly bold to drug her drink right here in a restaurant, with other diners around. What if the ladies' restroom had been occupied and she'd come right back to the table?

So she wasn't *too* concerned about her drink, although of course she was going to leave it untouched. A slight uneasy feeling and nothing more.

When they walked away from the table, she got frightened.

He hadn't taken his receipt.

How was he expensing this meal if he paid in cash and left his receipt behind? Did his investors work on the honor system? Business people dining with clients always wanted their receipts.

Eyes darting to her drink and an abandoned receipt weren't enough for her to point at him and scream *"Killer! Killer!"* But it was enough to scare her.

Was this the man who'd abducted Kimberly? Or was he just some guy who wanted to rape her? Or was she making a mistake?

She'd spent many hours walking the streets of Hornbeam Ridge after dark, hoping he'd show up to try to make her his prey. Now that he might very well be walking right next to her, she didn't think she wanted that at all. She wanted to be as far away from him as she could get.

Yet she did have her stun gun.

If he made a move, any move, she could zap the shit out of him and then make him tell her what he'd done with her cousin.

The smart plan would be to not walk out to the parking lot with him. Come up with an excuse to stay behind, then call the police. They might decide that she had too little to go on, but surely they would agree that the abductor had a motive to come after her. If she got back to the table before the server cleared it, she could turn her drink over to the authorities and let them test it.

Gertie knew what he looked like, though she suddenly thought the beard might be fake. She would be able to easily pick him out in a police lineup, but she might not be able to help create a police sketch that was good enough for them to catch him.

They'd exchanged e-mails. Surely he'd covered his tracks there. He wouldn't be dumb enough to communicate with a victim using an e-mail address that could be traced back to him.

What should she do? Surely she shouldn't just walk out of the restaurant with him. Yet if she pretended to have sudden stomach troubles and returned to the restroom, he'd get away and the police might not be able to find him. Kimberly was probably dead...but what if she wasn't?

The boldest option would be to zap him right here in the restaurant.

Yet what did she have to go on? He'd glanced at her drink and he didn't take his receipt. If he was innocent, she could be charged with assault. If you were going to slam a stun gun into somebody who'd made no aggressive moves toward you, you needed to be *very* sure he was really the bad guy.

She'd walk to the parking lot with him. Try to see his license plate. She had her purse over her right shoulder, and he was on her left side, so she casually unzipped it as they walked through the restaurant. If he tried anything at all, she'd zap him.

He took a mint from the bowl at the hostess's station and then held the door for her as she walked outside.

"Thanks for dinner," she said. "It was delicious. So you'll just e-mail me and we can take the next step?"

He nodded but didn't say anything.

She knew.

Ken had no idea how she'd figured it out. But Gertie was suddenly acting a bit nervous and weird, and though he'd like to believe that it was simply him being paranoid, he had to assume that she knew who he was.

Which meant that they absolutely could not part ways tonight.

JEFF STRAND

CHAPTER TEN

"Yes," Ken finally said. "I'll send you an e-mail with everything you need to know. The sooner we can make this happen the better, but of course we'll work with your schedule."

"Great. Well, I look forward to working with you." Gertie's voice had just a hint of a tremor. The bitch was doing an admirable job of pretending that everything was fine, but her act wasn't *quite* good enough to fool him.

He glanced around the parking lot. Nobody else was there. He didn't think an upscale seafood restaurant would bother to have cameras monitoring the parking lot. If he could get her quickly, he could do it without witnesses.

"Well, I'm over this way," Gertie said, pointing to the left.

"Me too," Ken lied. Gertie didn't look happy to hear that. He wasn't being paranoid. She knew something was wrong. And she'd have proof very, very soon.

He wondered if she'd be transparent enough to say, "Oh, no, wait, I was wrong, I'm over there," and point in the other direction. He hoped so. He liked the idea of her being so flustered and scared that she said really stupid shit.

"Okay," she said, walking away. He followed.

This was a mistake. She should've stayed in the restaurant.

She could pretend that one of these closer vehicles was hers, but if he didn't immediately go on his merry way, he'd see that she couldn't open the door and know she was lying.

So they kept walking. She actually had her hand in her purse, fingers wrapped around the stun gun, and she didn't care if he noticed.

What was she reaching for in her purse? Pepper spray? He'd have to be careful.

"Well, here I am," Gertie said, as they reached a small blue car, about what he'd expect a young waitress to drive.

He opened his arms. "Can I have a goodbye hug?"

Gertie looked very uncertain. "Oh, uh, yes, I guess, sure."

Ken put his arms around her.

If this creepy asshole was asking for a hug, Gertie didn't care if she was mistaken about him being a mass abductor. She had the right to protect herself.

He squeezed her tight. Too tight for a friendly hug.

She slammed the stun gun into his side.

It hurt like hell. Ken even let out a yelp.

If Ken believed in God, he'd have to believe that God was looking down and nodding with approval at what he was doing, because this had been one hell of a happy accident. He was wearing several layers of clothing. Not to protect himself against a chick with a stun gun, but to disguise his appearance, so that witnesses would remember him as a guy who could stand to spend a little more time on a treadmill.

His plan had been to hug her and whisper into her ear that if she wanted to see her cousin alive again, she'd have to come with him. If she reacted poorly, he'd quickly slam her into her car and try to knock her unconscious before anybody else came out of the restaurant. It was far from a foolproof plan, but he couldn't just let her leave.

When she got him with the stun gun—and she should *not* have been able to do that—and the pain shot through him he'd thought that this was it, it was over, he was going to prison. But the padding meant that all it did was hurt. It didn't incapacitate him.

He didn't want to cry out and alert anybody, so he twitched as if he was being electrocuted. He was sure it looked ridiculous, but he only needed to keep this performance going for a second.

He released the hug then grabbed Gertie's arm, the one with the stun gun. He spun her around and twisted her arm behind her back. Not hard enough to break any bones, but hard enough to send a jolt of pain through her.

Ken had to move quickly, before she screamed for help.

He wrenched the stun gun out of her hand then pressed it against the back of her neck.

She cried out. But it wasn't a scream—it was more of a loud grunt. It was unlikely that anybody inside the restaurant heard her.

Gertie's legs wobbled and she dropped to one knee.

Ken didn't want to kill her yet, but he couldn't take the risk of her shouting for help. He didn't know much about stun guns and wasn't sure how much damage a second hit would do to her. He had to take the risk. If she died, she died.

He pressed the stun gun against the back of her neck again. This time the crackling sound was louder than her grunt. Gertie pitched forward, arms and legs twitching. She was gasping for breath, so she wasn't dead.

The parking lot was still empty.

He had to move quickly. He bent over her and scooped her up into his arms. If she struggled too much, he'd shut that down by dropping her on her head, but she didn't move except for the twitching.

She wasn't very heavy. All he had to do was carry her to his car before anybody walked out of the restaurant. He didn't run, but he walked fast, feeling a definite sense of panic as he hurried to his vehicle.

Almost there...almost there...

He set her on the ground next to the passenger side of his car, then unlocked the door. His hands were shaking. This was an insane risk, but less of a risk than just letting her leave. He'd made it past the worst part. If somebody caught him now, he could offer a reasonably plausible explanation.

Ken opened the car door. Picked Gertie up and put her in the passenger seat. No time to fasten the seatbelt. He'd do that after they'd driven away from The Shellfish Grotto.

He heard the restaurant door open.

He froze as a couple walked outside.

No. Don't freeze. There was nothing suspicious about somebody getting in their car in a parking lot. That's what he was supposed to be doing. He just needed to behave like there was nothing wrong.

He closed the passenger's side door and walked around to the driver's side door, feeling weirdly conscious of every step he was taking, as if he was taking steps like a space alien that would draw undue attention. He opened the door, wondering if he was opening it in a normal manner, then got inside.

The couple was walking in the opposite direction. They hadn't noticed anything.

He took a deep breath to calm himself. Gertie was slumped over toward him, so he shoved her back toward her own door. Then he reclined her seat all the way back.

"Can you hear me?" he asked. "I hope so. I hope you know what's going on. It's going to be awful for you. Really fucking awful. Whatever nightmare is playing in your mind right now, it doesn't compare to the reality of what you're about to endure. I hope you realize that."

He shut off the stun gun and wedged it into the gap

between his seat and the door. Then he started the engine and backed out of the parking space. Nobody else came out of the restaurant, but it wouldn't matter if they did. There was no longer anything suspicious to see.

He drove away from the restaurant. He'd come back for her car tonight. She might have been lying about which vehicle was hers, but it didn't matter. Ken loved keyless entry, since it meant that all he had to do was click the button on her keychain and her car would beep and flash its headlights. No suspicious going from vehicle to vehicle, testing the locks.

A few blocks later, he pulled into the parking lot of a different restaurant. This one was closed and there were no other cars in the lot. He put the car into park, then patted Gertie's front pockets. No cell phone. Reaching under her ass, he found it. She probably had a passcode, but maybe he'd get lucky.

He got lucky.

He smiled as he scrolled through her text messages. Good to know she didn't think he was a sleazy weirdo.

Charlene picked up her phone as a text arrived from Gertie.

So....NOT on my way home. ☺

Charlene frowned and typed: *???*

Promise you won't think I'm a slut?

You're not going home with the producer, are you?

No! He's way too old. But our cute waiter isn't. ☺

All right. Have fun. Make him wear a condom, you godless tramp.

Yes, Mom. I'll share all of the details tomorrow.
I don't want any of them.
K bye.

Charlene set her phone back on the coffee table. She didn't think it was such a great idea for Gertie to be going home with a guy she'd just met, but Charlene wasn't her mother or her babysitter, and she couldn't claim that all of her sexual encounters involved lengthy courtships. At least she'd be safer banging some waiter than the way she *had* been spending her nights.

Ken shut off Gertie's phone, then crouched down and bashed it against the pavement. Phones were extremely well made these days and it took a lot of pounding to be sure the phone wasn't salvageable. Then he tossed it into the restaurant's Dumpster. She'd probably be more upset over the loss of her phone than being kidnapped.

He got back in the car and drove across town.

No sirens. No flashing lights. No sign that anybody was following him.

He'd gotten away with it. Vivian would crap her pants if she knew the risks he'd taken, but he'd done it. Gertie was his. Poor girl. If only she'd been able to tell that his layers of clothing weren't his natural blubber, she wouldn't be unconscious in his car right now.

He saw no reason to kill her and be done with it. She was going into one of the empty cages with the rest of his pretty ladies. Let her have plenty of time to suffer and reflect upon how she brought this upon herself. The other women weren't responsible for their own hellish fates, but as Gertie watched her body wither away she'd know that this was her fault.

Ken pulled into the driveway of the rental house. It was equipped with a remote controlled garage door opener, but no good could come from the device being found inside his car, so he'd have to go inside to open it.

Gertie was stirring a little. Just a little. He didn't want to shock her again, and the chloroform was hidden inside, so he'd have to leave her. It wouldn't even be a full minute. The most she could do was get the door open, tumble out onto the driveway, and crawl a couple of feet before he caught her.

Unless she was faking it.

"Hey, you awake?" he asked her.

Gertie didn't respond.

Ken picked up the stun gun, but left it turned off. "I'm going to shock you again, so brace yourself." Though no electricity was flowing, there'd be some sort of reaction unless she was the best actor in the world. "Three, two, *one.*" He pressed it against the back of her neck. Gertie didn't even flinch. She wasn't faking—she was still mostly out of it.

He left her in the car as he unlocked the door to the garage. He went inside, turned on the light, walked over to the far end, and pressed the button. As the door slowly lifted, he had a mental image of Gertie sprinting away, but when he returned to the vehicle she was still barely conscious in the passenger seat.

He got back into the car, pulled into the garage, then got out and pressed the button to close the door again.

Ken sighed with relief as the bottom of the garage door hit the cement. Now he had complete privacy. He sat there for a few moments, breathing deeply. He hadn't realized just how tense he'd been since dessert. But it was all good now.

Though he didn't think Gertie would give him any problems, he didn't want to be an idiot about it, so he went to retrieve the chloroform so he could knock her out completely. Then he poured some onto the rag and pressed it against her face.

He couldn't wait to see her expression when she woke up.

He carried her down to the basement.

Olivia was still alive, so Gertie would have some company, though Olivia wasn't *good* company, not anymore.

Getting the cage down was pretty easy. He climbed the stepladder, unfastened the locking mechanism at the top, and then slowly gave slack to the chain as the cage lowered to the floor.

Then he unlocked the front of the cage, swung it open, and gently placed Gertie inside her forever home. He locked it back up.

The hard part was getting the cage back up to the ceiling, since the already heavy cage was now even heavier, and he had to raise it instead of lowering it. He wished he had an automatic spooling system or at least a lever, but no, he basically just had to pull on the chain until the cage was high enough for the locking mechanism to spring shut.

But he got it up there, then took a few moments to admire his work.

The date rape drugs had to wear off on their own, but since Gertie had been chloroformed he could wake her up with smelling salts. He retrieved them, climbed back up the ladder, and waved them underneath Gertie's nose.

Her eyes popped open.

"Hi," he said.

Gertie looked like she was going to start screaming, but Ken placed his index finger to his lips and she didn't make a sound. She simply stared at him with wide-eyed terror. Then she began to cough as the reek of death hit her.

"This is where you're going to die," he informed her. "It's going to take a long time. I don't have much of anything else to say."

He climbed back down the ladder.

"Wait!" said Gertie. "Please, wait!"

"Oh, I bet you're wondering where your cousin is. Kimberly, right? She's right over there. There are a couple of cages between you two, so you won't be able to see her, but I think you'll believe me when I say that's for the best. People don't look good after they're dead and rotting."

Gertie let out a sob. Ken assumed she was crying more for herself than for her cousin's tragic demise, but he supposed it could be a little of both. He'd briefly considered giving her a spot right next to Kimberly's corpse, then decided that he didn't want to swap out the bodies. Kimberly might fall apart in the process.

"My friend is—"

"Your friend thinks that you're getting laid at this very moment. That would be way better, wouldn't it? Crouched on your hands and knees, getting it from behind? Sorry to say those days are over. All you get to do now is sit in your little cage and wait to die. No food. Not a crumb. If you'd minded your own business, maybe you *would* be having doggy-style sex with a hot waiter right now."

"Please! People will be looking for me!"

"I know. All of your roommates said the same thing. Nobody found them."

Gertie tried not to succumb to complete blind panic. She had to stay calm. Make him see reason. She couldn't keep the tears from flowing, but as long as she could keep herself from simply squeezing her eyes shut and screaming at the top of her lungs, maybe she could talk her way out of this.

Ken picked up the stepladder and walked out of sight. A moment later he walked back to where Gertie could see him.

"I wish I could stay longer," he said. "I'll be back tomorrow, though."

"Listen to me," said Gertie, keeping her voice as steady as possible. "You can't get away with this. I'll be found."

"I disagree with that."

"They can track me."

"Is that so?"

She nodded. "It's a GPS tracker."

"I didn't see one when I searched you. Are you saying that it's an implant?"

"Yes. I had it put in when I went out looking for you. They'll trace me back here. But if you let me go, I'll leave and I won't say a word, I promise."

"Really? It's too late for your dead cousin, but you won't try to save your neighbor Olivia? She's still alive." He pointed to the woman in the cage next to hers.

Kimberly's death was not a surprise and Gertie forced herself not to let it distract her. She tried to think of the proper way to answer this. "I don't know her."

"That's pretty cold-blooded."

"I just want to go home."

"If you have a tracker implant, then I guess I'll have to lop off whatever part of you has it. Is it your arm? One of your legs? What about your head? Or should I just completely dismember you to be sure?"

Gertie didn't answer. She rested her forehead against the cage and wept.

"Lucky for you, I know you're lying, so I won't have to start chopping off limbs. I'll be back tomorrow. You can have some water then. But I hope you enjoyed the chocolate cake, because that was your final meal."

She said nothing as he left.

It wasn't hopeless. When people finally realized that she'd gone missing, her picture would be on the news, and Charlene would tell the police that Gertie had been at The Shellfish Grotto before she disappeared. Their server would remember the guy she'd been with. The cops would find him, and force him to reveal where he kept his kidnapping victims.

Easy, right?

That's why she was in a basement full of corpses.

Ken felt great as he locked the door. He got her. She'd thought she was smarter than him, and he'd bested her. She was going to die a slow, agonizing death, simply because she'd tried to mess with the wrong guy. He was positively ecstatic.

He went upstairs, then locked the second door. He really wished he had more time tonight—he was certain that Gertie was down there freaking the hell out. He'd thought about installing a webcam, but wasn't positive that he could make the feed completely secure.

If he'd ever learned to whistle, this was when he'd use that skill. He couldn't remember the last time he'd been this upbeat. None of the other abductions had given him this much satisfaction.

Was it the extra element of danger?

Or was it because Gertie was more personal than the others? She was trying to harm him. She actually deserved her fate.

He supposed it didn't matter. He wasn't going to start purposely trying to make his abductions more dangerous, and if revenge became part of his victim selection, he'd eventually get caught, no doubt about it.

So he'd simply enjoy feeling good while it lasted. He doubted it would be long.

Ken walked into the garage and pressed the button to open the door. He got into his car, turned on the engine, and made a failed attempt to whistle as he waited for the door to raise all the way. After it did, he put the car into reverse, backed out—and immediately slammed on the brakes to avoid hitting the person who'd stepped into view.

Vivian. Not looking happy.

CHAPTER ELEVEN

Ken just stared into the rearview mirror, trying not to shit his pants.

She walked over to his door. It took him a moment to think to put the vehicle in park. He rolled down the window, accidentally using the lever for the back window first, then correcting his mistake.

"Get out of the car," Vivian told him.

Ken opened the door.

"Shut off the engine first."

He shut off the engine, pocketed the keys, and got out of the car. He shut the door, removed the keys from his pocket to lock the car, then shoved the keys back into his pocket again. His stomach hurt and he wanted to hurry over to the bushes and vomit. Instead, he stood his ground.

"Why are you here?" he asked.

"I've got a better question," said Vivian. "Why are *you* here?"

"Did you follow me?"

"No. I put Jared's phone under your seat. Tracked it with the computer. And that's the only question I'll be answering until you explain whose house this is."

Ken wanted to be outraged at the invasion of privacy, the lack of trust...but her lack of trust had been justified, so what could he say?

She probably thought he was having an affair. And Ken honestly wasn't sure if she'd react worse to that, or to the caged women in the basement.

"It's nobody's house," he said. It was the stupidest thing he could have possibly said, but his mind was a Tilt-a-Whirl right now.

"Nobody's house," Vivian repeated.

Ken shrugged.

"Is she inside?"

"Who?"

"Don't you dare pretend that you don't know what I'm talking about! Is she inside? I'm not going to hurt her. I'm just going to tell her to stay the hell away from you."

"She's not inside."

"Bullshit." Vivian stormed into the garage. Ken hurriedly followed her.

She tried to open the door to the inside. When the knob wouldn't turn, she began to pound on the door.

"Nobody's inside," Ken said.

"Fucking liar!" Vivian pounded on the door even harder. "Open up! Open the fuck up!"

"Quiet!" Ken said. "The neighbors will hear."

"You think I care?" She continued to pound on the door.

"I said, nobody's inside."

"Then unlock the door."

"I don't have a key."

"Do you want me to search you?"

Defeated, Ken took out the key and unlocked the door. Before he'd even pulled the key out of the lock, Vivian opened the door and walked inside. Ken considered the possibility of jumping in his car, speeding off, and leaving his entire life behind, but he followed her instead.

If she went into Darrell's room, she'd see all of the sex toys, and there'd be no way to convince her that they didn't belong to him. He didn't think Darrell would show up to serve as a character witness.

But she didn't. She stopped at the door to the staircase. She tapped the passcode display.

"What's down there?" she asked.

"I don't know."

"Why does it have a high-tech lock like this?"

"I don't know."

"Ken, I'm going to find out what's behind this door. You can show me yourself, or I can go down there with a locksmith. Which do you want?"

"Can't we talk about this?"

Vivian shook her head so violently that he thought she might hurt her neck. "No, because you keep lying. Unlock the door. Unlock it now."

Ken punched in the four-digit code. Vivian opened the door and walked down the stairs.

"Are you fucking kidding me?" she asked as she reached the second door and the second passcode lock.

"Let me explain first," said Ken.

"I don't want you to explain. I want you to open the door."

"It's going to be upsetting."

"Yeah, I figured that out when we got to the second goddamn locked door."

There would be no dissuading her from this. He could, in theory, use the stun gun on her, but she was his wife and he'd never physically harm her. Not ever. He'd never laid a hand on her, and he never would.

He tried to think of some explanation he could offer, something to cushion the blow of what she was about to see, but he came up blank. What could he possibly say that would make these next few moments less horrifying?

Ken punched in the code. The door unlocked.

"It's going to smell bad," he said. "Brace yourself."

He opened the door.

The putrid scent hit Vivian so hard that she immediately doubled over and vomited. She stood back up, coughing and spitting and wiping tears out of her eyes.

Then she stepped inside the room.

She clasped her hand over her mouth as she gazed around at the cages.

Dropped to her knees.

"Please!" Gertie shouted. "You have to help me!"

Ken walked over and slammed the bottom of her cage with his fist. "You shut up! Say another word and I'll skin you alive! I'll take bites out of your fucking stomach! You understand me?"

Without waiting for her to respond, he returned to Vivian. He took her by the hand and tried to help her up.

"C'mon, Viv. You've seen it now. Let's leave, okay?"

Vivian pulled her hand away, then slapped at his hand when he tried again. She got up on her own, then staggered out of the room. Ken went after her, closing and locking the door behind them.

She sat down on the stairs, breathing like she'd just finished running a marathon. She wiped her mouth with the back of her hand then wiped it on the stair. Finally she looked up at Ken.

"You said you strangled them."

"I know."

"You lied to me."

Ken nodded. He was suddenly very self-conscious of his hands. He put them behind his back and just stood there. Vivian was silent for an excruciatingly long time.

"I need to understand this," she said. "Tell me what you get out of this."

"I'm not sure I can explain it."

"Try."

Ken looked at the floor. "I don't know."

"You don't know? What are you, seven years old?"

"It's not something I can articulate! What, you think I can just give you a quick summary of why I did this?"

"It doesn't need to be a quick summary. Take all the time you need. I'm not going anywhere."

"I...I can't. It won't make sense." Ken's cheeks were burning and sweat trickled down his sides. He'd taken great precautions to avoid ever having to have this conversation with Vivian. He felt sick to his stomach and ashamed. Once again he considered running away. Pushing past her, running up the stairs, and getting as far away as he possibly could.

Would she let him go? Would she call the cops?

One thing was for sure: he'd never see Jared again. And he'd rather go down in a hail of police gunfire than lose his son. He wouldn't take his own life like that dumbass who'd turned Charlene and Gertie into heroes, but he wouldn't go easily.

"We're not leaving this house until we've finished this conversation," said Vivian. "I don't care how long it takes. So you can either use your grown-up words and explain to me why you keep women in cages, or we can sit here until we get caught."

Ken assumed she was bluffing. If she wasn't, the worst-case scenario is that Darrell would show up, and Ken could get rid of him pretty easily. Still, this wasn't going to get any easier, so he might as well try to get it over with.

He tried to think of a credible lie, but couldn't come up with one that made him sound any less deranged than the truth.

"I'm sorry that I told you I strangled them," he said, figuring that starting off with an apology was a good first step. "I shouldn't have lied. The truth is that I do this because it's...because it's *worse* for them. It's longer. I just like to watch them while they slowly fade away. I like coming back each time and seeing how much more their bodies have wasted away. I like how awful it must be for them." Now that he was finally articulating it, this was easier than he'd expected.

Vivian just stared at him, expressionless.

"A strangling is over in a minute. It can take weeks to starve to death."

"You don't give them any food at all?"

Ken shook his head. "Water but no food."

"And you don't do anything to them? You just leave them in the cages?"

"Right."

"Okay." Vivian was silent for a moment. "You understand why I have a problem with this, right?"

"Yeah."

"I had no idea you were this sadistic. This is seriously disturbed behavior, Ken. How do you even pay for this place? For the cages?"

Ken decided that he might as well continue telling the truth. "That time I came home furious because I wasn't getting a raise? That was a lie. It was a good raise."

Vivian let out a long sigh. "What other lies have you told? Let's just get it all out there."

"That's it. I lied about my raise and I lied about what I did to the women, but that's it."

Vivian didn't respond. She sat there for a while. Ken wasn't sure if she was waiting for him to speak, or trying to think of what she wanted to say. He just stood there, perspiring.

She wiped a tear from her eye and stood up. "Don't you ever lie to me again," she said.

"I won't. I swear."

"If you do, I will leave you."

"I know. I'm done with the lies. They're over."

"All right."

"So what are we going to do about this?" Ken asked. "I'll do whatever you want."

"How many women are still alive?"

"Two."

"I want you to kill them. Right now."

"Oh."

"You just said you'd do whatever I want. Are you now saying that you don't want to kill them?"

Ken shook his head. "No, no."

"Do you agree that it's the right thing to do?"

"I guess."

"You told me that you were killing them quickly and burying them in a shallow grave. Instead I find that you're keeping them locked in cages in a basement for weeks. That's a hell of a lot more risk for you, which

145

means it's a hell of a lot more risk for me. Finish them off. We'll take it from there."

"How?"

"I don't care how. Strangle them like you said you did. Stick a fucking knife in their head. It doesn't matter. Just do it."

Ken really didn't want to do this, especially not with Olivia so close to passing away on her own, but he knew better than to argue. "I'll get a knife from upstairs," he said.

He walked past Vivian and opened the top door. The way things were going tonight, it wouldn't have surprised him to see Darrell waiting up there, but the upstairs was still empty. He went into the kitchen, unsure if there were any utensils actually available. He'd never prepared a meal in this house, though he assumed Darrell had shared a snack with at least one of his mistresses.

He opened a couple of drawers and found one with forks, spoons, and knives. He selected a pretty good steak knife. Ken wouldn't use it for one-on-one combat, but it should do the trick against a helpless girl locked in a cage.

He shut the drawer and leaned against the counter. He couldn't believe how badly he'd messed things up. He should've realized how suspicious Vivian was getting and been more careful. Hell, as much of an idiot as he'd been, he deserved to starve to death in one of those cages himself.

He walked back downstairs, shutting the door behind him.

"Pretty small knife," she said.

"House didn't come with butcher knives."

Vivian cupped her hands over her nose and mouth as

Ken punched in the code. He opened the door just a bit, waiting for the smell to waft over them.

"Do you want to watch or...?"

"I'll wait here."

"Okay." Ken walked into the room with the cages, and closed the door.

Warren looked shaken and grim as he entered the room, holding a knife.

"Listen to me," said Gertie. "I know how we can work this out."

He ignored her and walked past her cage.

"I've got money," she called out after him. "I'd signed a non-disclosure agreement so I couldn't tell you before, but I got a ton of money for the movie rights to my story. It's enough for me to disappear. I can buy a new identity. I'll leave the country and you'll never hear from me again."

Warren returned with a stepladder. He set it next to the cage of the other woman who seemed to still be alive, if only barely.

"I know a guy," Gertie insisted. "He can make it happen right away."

Warren glared at her. "Is that the best you could come up with? I don't even go to movies, and I know that you wouldn't have a check already."

"It's coming. Direct deposit. I'll have the money any minute now."

"Just shut up, all right? Don't talk to me. You're being put out of your misery, so if anything you should be grateful."

He climbed to the top of the ladder.

It took a moment for Olivia to feel scared.

Her eyes wouldn't quite focus, though she realized that he had a knife, and though she wanted nothing more than to be free of this prison she wasn't ready to die. She wanted to be rescued. Somebody should have rescued her by now. Somebody should have kicked down the door.

Olivia wanted to move her head away from the blade, but she couldn't make her neck work. Nor could she speak to beg him to stop.

She couldn't feel anything.

Had he started killing her yet?

Then she felt a sharp sting in her left ear. He'd shoved the knife in, deep enough to hurt, deep enough to make her bleed, but not deep enough to kill her. She didn't know if he was purposely drawing it out to scare her, or if he was hesitating because he didn't want to go through with it.

She hoped he didn't kill her.

Even if she died in this cage, she didn't want to die now.

A sudden intense pain. And then nothing.

Gertie screamed.

Some blood dribbled onto the cement floor—not much—and then Warren climbed down the ladder. He moved it over to Gertie's cage.

There was no way she could fight him off. But she was damn well going to try. Getting slashed up by him would be a much worse way to go than simply letting him shove a blade into her brain, but she didn't care. She was going to resist this asshole until she was free or until she was dead.

Warren climbed up the ladder.

"Get the hell away from me," Gertie told him.

"Don't resist. It'll be a lot worse for you if you resist."

"Then it'll have to be a lot worse for me."

She kicked at the ladder. He slammed the knife into her upper thigh, plunging in deep. Gertie cried out in pain, then cried out again as he wrenched the knife free. He held up the bloody blade.

"Do *not* make this difficult," he said, spittle flying from his mouth.

Gertie kicked at the ladder with her other leg. He plunged the blade into that leg, yanked it out, then stabbed her again in the same spot.

"What the fuck is the matter with you?" he asked. "You lucked out by having her show up! Do you really want to go through the hell on earth that the other women suffered? Are you that stupid?"

She heard a patter as drops of her blood hit the floor.

"You're not going to kill me," she informed him.

He slammed the knife through the bars. It missed her ear and tore across her cheek. She grabbed the blade but couldn't get a solid grip on it as he pulled it away, slashing open her palm. More blood dripped onto the floor.

The door opened.

"Ken! Wait!" said the woman. What had he called her? Viv?

This should have been the moment where Warren—Ken—looked over at her, and Gertie took advantage of his split-second of distraction to kick him off the ladder, where he'd splatter his head onto the cement. But he didn't look away from her. He simply climbed down the ladder.

Gertie was too frightened to be relieved.

Viv looked at the tiny pool of blood underneath the newly dead woman's cage. Then she looked over at Gertie.

"Did he rape you?" she asked.

Gertie wasn't sure what the correct answer was, so she went with the truth. "No."

"Did you fuck him?"

Gertie shook her head.

Viv turned her attention to Ken. "You can keep her," she said.

"Seriously?"

"Yes. But I'm not going to let you sit here surrounded by shit and piss and puke. That's mentally ill. You're going to clean up the floor, and I mean clean it *good*, with bleach, and then you're going to start moving the corpses out. Not all at once, but I want them gone within a week. She can stay until she's dead. Does that work for you?"

Ken vigorously nodded. "Yes. Yes, it absolutely works for me."

"Are there cleaning supplies upstairs?"

"Yes, in the garage, I think."

"Then do it now. I'll wait upstairs. I can't take the smell any more."

Viv left the room. Ken moved the stepladder several feet away from Gertie's cage. He wasn't smiling, but he looked intensely relieved.

With the threat of imminent death gone, Gertie could focus on her wounds. The pain in her legs was excruciating and the blood was still flowing. Same with her palm. She could feel several trickles of blood running down her cheek. If this had happened at home, she wouldn't be worried about bleeding to death before she could receive medical attention, but up here in a cage...

"Are you going to patch me up?" she asked.

"Hell no."

"I can't starve to death if I bleed to death first."

Ken flipped her the bird as he walked out of the room.

Surely he wouldn't just leave her like this. Gertie had no idea how long it would take her to bleed out, but if he didn't at least give her something to wrap up her legs she wouldn't last the night.

He returned a few minutes later with a mop, a bucket of water, and a large plastic jar of bleach. He dumped the mop into the bucket and began to clean up the floor.

Ken had to change the mop water several times before he was done with the floor. During the process he didn't say a word to Gertie. Then he mopped the floor with bleach. He looked around, apparently satisfied with a job well done.

He left the room again. A moment later, he returned with Viv.

She put her hand over her nose. "I can still smell the rot."

Ken nodded. "Yeah, bleach isn't going to cover it completely. But it'll fade after I get the bodies out of here."

Viv pointed to the floor underneath Gertie's cage. "She's already getting more blood on the floor. Do you have any bandages or gauze or anything?"

"Small bandages. Nothing big enough for stab wounds."

"If you want to keep her alive longer, you can go get some. Or not. It's up to you."

"I'll patch her up."

"You should probably do it soon."

"There's a twenty-four hour Wal-Mart near here."

"All right. I have to get out of here."

Viv left the room. Ken followed her, closing the door behind him.

"Thank you," said Ken, as they walked up the stairs. "I'm so sorry for lying to you. I just didn't think you'd understand."

"I *don't* understand. I accept it but I don't understand it."

"That's fair. That's totally fair. I just want to say thank you."

"You're welcome."

They walked into the main part of the house. Ken wondered if Viv had been wandering around. If so, she would've seen Darrell's room. Based on the fact that she hadn't said, "What the hell is all of this stuff?" he assumed that she hadn't gone snooping.

"You do know what this means, right?" Viv asked.

"What?"

"I get to do one."

CHAPTER TWELVE

Charlene stood in the shower, massaging coconut-scented shampoo through her hair, reliving the moment when Lee pulled the trigger.

It was more violent in the mental replay. The real alley had been dark. She hadn't seen the bullet burst through the back of his skull. But in her mind, everything was brightly lit, like a fluorescent bulb during a power surge. She saw blood—more blood than medically possible—and chunks of brain matter and shards of skull, all flying through the air like a high-definition 3-D motion picture in super-slow motion. When Lee struck the ground, his head splattered apart like a Jack-o-Lantern left on the front porch for an extra week by somebody who wasn't willing to let Halloween go. The flow of blood was endless. And Lee was still alive. He lay on the ground, writhing in the pool of blood, staring at her with frightened eyes that bulged from their sockets.

Charlene wished this were a dream. She wished it were only her subconscious mind conjuring up these awful images. She didn't need this shit while she was awake, trying to enjoy a relaxing hot shower.

She rinsed her hair while Lee clawed at his own mangled head, moaning in agony.

She got out of the shower and toweled off. Things had gotten better since the incident, but she still had these nightmarish moments when she was alone.

The simple solution was to not be alone. Her parents would happily let her stay with them. But she worried that if she hid from her apartment for a few days, she might return and go straight back to where she'd left off. Better to just start facing the demons now.

She didn't really want any kind of long-term relationship with Megan, so using her as emotional cover seemed like a bad idea. Charlene most definitely did not regret the sex, but that was to blow off steam, not to keep herself out of her own head.

She'd love to call Gertie, just to talk for a little bit, since she had the closest understanding to what Charlene had been through. But of course Gertie was getting laid right now. Gertie hadn't really seemed like the kind of person who'd go home with somebody she'd just met, especially when she was at the restaurant as part of a business meeting. It felt a little out of character, but Charlene hadn't known Gertie for very long and had not asked for details about her heterosexual love life. For all she knew, it was ridiculously easy to get into Gertie's pants. Gertie was a young, healthy woman, and she could bang whomever she wanted. More power to her. It was none of Charlene's business.

She suddenly wondered if the sexual promiscuity was the only reason it felt a bit off.

Charlene picked up her phone and glanced at the text message conversation again.

No! He's way too old. But our cute waiter isn't. ☺

Waiter.

She'd never heard Gertie use the words "waiter" or "waitress." They were servers.

That didn't necessarily mean Gertie *wouldn't* use the word "waiter" in a text message. Maybe she wanted to use a gender-specific term when conveying the message to her lesbian friend.

Charlene texted her back: *Hey, feeling a little uneasy here. Check in, okay?*

She waited. No response.

She took her phone with her as she went into the kitchen and popped a bag of microwave popcorn. Still no answer as she poured it into the bowl.

Okay, if there was an appropriate time for somebody to not check their text messages, it was when they were having sex. Even if he was pounding into her doggy-style and she could conveniently hold her phone without interrupting the flow too much, it would be rude.

Screw it. She was going to call, even if she was interrupting Gertie and the server in the throes of passionate lovemaking.

It went straight to voice mail.

Not suspicious. Charlene had put her own phone on Do Not Disturb mode when Megan's head was between her legs.

She called again, just in case Gertie had the setting where a second call from the same number would go through.

Straight to voice mail.

Even Sherlock Holmes might suggest that "waiter" versus "server" was a bit of a stretch. So, again, this wasn't suspicious.

But she couldn't deny that it was a bit troubling.

"Excuse me?" Ken asked.

"You know you heard me."

"Tell me again."

"I get to do one."

Ken felt a little sick to his stomach. Not the gut-churning sensation he'd felt when Vivian had forced him to show her the basement, but sick nevertheless.

"I thought you got that out of your system before we met."

"I did. And now I want to do it again."

"I don't think it's a good idea."

"Why?"

"You could get caught."

Vivian let out a snort of laughter. "You've got a basement full of girls in cages. I'm going to go out on a great big old limb and say that I'd be at less risk of getting caught than you."

Ken shook his head. "I don't want that."

"Then maybe you shouldn't have lied about what a deviant you are. You get your girls. I get my man. That's fair."

"I know, but..."

"But you're okay with a double standard?"

"It's different."

"How?"

Ken had no good answer for that. "I thought you said you weren't interested in that anymore."

"I wasn't. Now I am. People change. And sometimes they aren't what they pretend to be."

Damn it. This had been going so well for a while.

"Didn't you fuck them before you killed them?" Ken asked.

"Yes."

"Is that still part of the deal?"

"I haven't decided."

"Well, it's a pretty important part."

"Again, you've got *eight or nine women in cages in a basement.* Fucking a guy then stabbing him to death doesn't come anywhere close."

"I wasn't allowed to rape them."

"I wouldn't be raping him."

"I wasn't allowed to have consensual sex with them."

"I get that."

"So you're the one with the double standard."

"Maybe," said Vivian. "But your double standard is infinitely worse."

"I wouldn't say infinitely."

"I would."

"No. I'm not going to let you do that."

"I won't have sex with him, then. I'll lure him with the promise, but I won't go through with it."

"How far will you go?"

"I don't know."

"I need to know that."

"Let me be clear about something," said Vivian. "I didn't say that I *want* one of my own. I said that I *get* one of my own. You betrayed my trust in a big way. You put our whole family at risk. You made it so Jared could lose his father. So if it means that now I get to do something that makes you uncomfortable, well, you should have thought about that before you lived out your sickest fantasies without telling me."

"So...a random guy?"

"Maybe not. We need to talk to your prisoner and find out what loose ends might be out there. She might have told her friend where she was going tonight. And somebody who looks like her probably has a boyfriend. We'll get them out of the picture before she's been reported missing."

"What if you killed the other girl instead?" Ken asked.

"Why? So you could watch?"

"No! I just think it's a better way to handle it."

"I don't want to kill her. That does nothing for me. You're lucky I didn't run screaming to the police, so I'm not sure why you're being a baby about this."

Ken's whole body tensed up. "Are you threatening to go to the cops?"

"Of course I'm not. I'd never do that to you or Jared. And I'd do some jail time, too, because I knew you were responsible for the disappearances. But that doesn't mean that, in an emotional state, I wouldn't have done something without thinking. You should be so goddamn relieved right now that you wouldn't care if I went out to a bar and started holding auditions for a gang-bang."

"Are you being serious right now?"

"I'm exaggerating. The basic point holds true. I don't get why you're upset about this idea even if I *did* fuck the guy."

"We should talk about this later."

"That's fine. You go get some antiseptic and bandages."

"She probably needs stitches," said Ken.

"Do you know how to do stitches?"

"No."

"Do you think she'll sit there and let you stitch her up without trying to escape?"

"I was going to chloroform her. Give me some credit."

"All right, I apologize," said Vivian. "Go get the things you need. I'm going to get some information out of her."

"How?"

"I'll be persuasive."

"Seriously, how?"

"Knife blade under the fingernails."

"Jesus."

"It's a time-tested method of getting people to share information they might not want to share. You think she can withstand torture like that?"

"You have to be careful on the ladder. Actually, no, I'll lower the cage. The door is padlocked shut. She won't get out."

"Perfect."

Gertie didn't say anything as Ken and Viv returned. She was starting to feel dizzy, but forced herself to stay alert, in case there was an opportunity to escape. Yeah. Escape from her locked steel cage dangling from the ceiling.

Ken walked past her. Viv stood by the doorway, holding the same knife that Ken had stabbed her with. She hadn't wiped off the blood.

The cage slowly began to lower.

Were they setting her free?

No, of course they weren't.

Gertie extended her legs so they wouldn't get crushed underneath the cage as it reached the floor.

Ken returned to the doorway. "Call me if you need anything," he said. "I won't be gone long." He gave Viv a kiss on the cheek then left.

Viv stood there for about a minute. Then she stepped forward and pulled the door closed.

"How can you stand the smell?" she asked. "I wish we could do this someplace else, but then you wouldn't be in a cage, would you?"

She walked over to the cage, though she didn't get close enough that Gertie could grab or kick her.

"I'm not going to start with a question," she said. "I'm going to start by showing you what happens if you don't answer a question. That way, when I do ask you a question, you'll know the penalty. Put your hand out."

"No."

"You're in a cage that barely gives you enough room to breathe. Do you really think that I can't get to you? When I say 'Put your hand out' what I mean is 'Put your hand out, because that's the easiest and least painful way for us to get through this.' The more difficult you make it for me, the more horrible I'll make it for you. And if I have to jab this knife into your ear like what happened to your friend over there, I'll do it. I have no emotional investment in keeping you alive."

Gertie could not see a way out of this. She couldn't extend her right arm, but she was able to get her hand outside of the cage.

Viv crouched down next to her. She grabbed Gertie by the wrist.

"Open your fist," Viv said.

"Please," said Gertie, amazed that she wasn't sobbing

yet. "I'll answer whatever questions you have."

"Really? Even if it puts your friends in danger? You'd sell them out to spare yourself a little pain?"

"You don't have to do this."

"I know I don't. I am *completely* aware of my options right now. Like my option to slash your wrist if you don't open your hand. I'm pretty sure you'll bleed to death before my husband gets back with the Band-Aids."

Gertie opened her hand.

Viv let go of Gertie's wrist and grabbed her pinky. She pressed the tip of the knife underneath her fingernail, then jammed it in, just a bit. Gertie shrieked as the pain shot all the way up her arm, so much worse than she ever could have anticipated.

Viv pulled the knife right out, but the pain took a while to fade. Gertie pulled her hand back inside the cage.

"So now you've had a sneak preview of what's going to happen if you don't cooperate. I'm going to ask you some questions. Don't lie to me. I'll know if you lie."

"The way you knew your husband was lying?"

Viv's face went dark and furious. Gertie didn't care. The woman clearly had every intention of torturing her, so why not piss her off? She might make a mistake.

Then the anger faded and Viv smiled. "Good one. Perceptive. You got me. No way for me to deny it, you got me, fair and square. But I'd like to get to the questions, if that's all right with you."

Gertie said nothing.

"Who knows where you were tonight?"

Gertie's phone had been gone when she regained consciousness, so Ken had almost certainly looked at it and probably seen her text messages. It would be stupid to lie. "My friend Charlene."

"Ah, the other amazing hero. And was Ms. Charlene expecting to hear from you again tonight?"

Now she was going to lie. She looked Viv directly in the eye. "No."

"Hmmm."

"We thought your husband wanted to interview me for a web series. There are a lot of sleazy people out there pretending to be producers, so I checked in with her to let her know that he wasn't a scumbag. I had no reason to text her after that."

"All right. Do you have a boyfriend?"

"No."

"Why not?"

"I broke up with my ex three months ago and haven't met anybody since then."

"Hmmm."

"It's true."

"I didn't say I didn't believe you. What about Charlene? Is there a man in her life?"

"No."

Viv looked unconvinced. "Both of you are single, huh?"

"Yes."

"Give me your hand."

"I'm telling the truth."

"Give me your hand."

"Charlene isn't into men. She'll never have a boyfriend."

"You should have clarified that when I asked the question. I'm going to consider that withholding information. Give me your hand."

"Fuck you."

Viv smiled. "Oh, well, if you use the F-word with me I have no choice but to back off, huh? I'm so intimidated by the little girl in the cage that I'll just let her decide if she takes a knife blade under the fingernail or not. You know, it doesn't have to be like the first time. I can stick that knife in all the way up to your knuckle. Is that how you'd like this to play out?"

"I didn't lie to you."

"And I'm being honest with you when I say this: I don't care. Give me your hand."

Now the tears were flowing. Gertie put her hand back outside of the cage.

Viv did not jam the knife in all the way up to the knuckle of her ring finger, but she didn't withdraw the blade as quickly as before. It took several moments for Gertie to stop shrieking.

"Tell me about the men in your life," said Viv. "Is your father still alive?"

"Yes."

"Does he live close?"

"No."

"Anybody at work? Attractive co-worker? Boss?"

"Fuck you. I'm not sending you after anyone."

"I like the defiance. If I were a lesbian like your friend it would be a real turn-on. You realize that I can very easily find this information out with a quick online search, right? It'll take almost no effort to find out who'll be the first man to miss you when you don't come home. So why not make things easy for yourself and tell me?"

"Go to hell," said Gertie.

"I'm sure there are pliers in the garage. I can loosen up your fingernails with the knife and then tear them off."

"I said, go to hell."

"All right. If that's the way you want to play it, that's fine with me. So you figured it out, huh?"

"Figured what out?"

"Figured out that I don't really need any of your answers. Like I said, I can find all of this online. And then pay a little visit to your place of employment. Have some fun. And since you've figured out that I don't need your answers, you've figured out that the part of the interrogation that I like is the part where I ruin your hands. So let's skip the Q&A and get to the good stuff."

Vivian was sitting on the upstairs couch when Ken walked into the house.

"Did she give you what you needed?" he asked.

Vivian shrugged. "She gave me enough."

"I got some antiseptic, some bandages, some gauze, and a needle and thread. I'll sew her up as well as I can, unless you want to do it."

"I'll pass."

He went downstairs and into the basement room. Gertie was slumped forward in her cage, eyes vacant. If not for the rise and fall of her chest, he would've thought she was dead. When Ken went over to the cage, he saw that the tips of all ten of her fingers were bloody.

Wow. That bitch must've been seriously uncooperative.

Ken poured some chloroform onto a rag, then reached through the bars and shoved it against Gertie's face. It didn't seem to make a difference, but he sure wasn't going to let her escape by something like faking catatonia.

Sewing up her stab wounds had gone horribly. The gashes were a mess of thread, but they seemed to be holding together well enough to keep her from bleeding too much. Ken was under no illusion that she'd live long enough to starve to death, but as long as the wounds didn't get infected—and they might, because once he raised the cage he wasn't lowering it again—she'd probably be around for at least a couple more days.

He shut the door, entered the passcode, then went back upstairs.

Vivian was still on the couch. "How's she doing?" she asked.

"Not great. That's pretty awful what you did to her fingers."

"She's lucky I didn't feel like tracking down a pair of pliers."

"But you got the information out of her?"

"I know my next step, yes."

"And that is...?"

"Are those your toys in the bedroom?"

"No," said Ken. "They're not. I promise they're not. They belong to my friend Darrell. He pays most of the rent on this place."

"Do we need to DNA test them to be sure?"

"I'm not lying."

"I know. I'm messing with you, sweetie. Will Darrell mind if we borrow some of them?"

"I assume so."

"Do you care if he minds?"

"Not at all. We'll wash them."

"Let's go."

CHAPTER THIRTEEN

Ken sat at his desk at work, a little sore but feeling good. He'd been *very* sore when he moved Gertie's car out of the parking lot last night and disposed of it.

Vivian had called in sick to her own job, so she could do a "research trip." She'd promised him that it was for the acquisition of information only. They'd discuss the next step together.

Travis sat in his favorite coffee shop, playing a word game on his phone while he sipped his espresso. The place was a lot more crowded in the morning than when he usually got here, but he wanted to run some errands before he opened the restaurant. At least he'd been able to find a table. He'd woken up to an e-mail from the attorney of the woman whom Charlene had dumped lasagna on, saying that she was suing for mental distress, but he'd decided to worry about that after he got a nice big dose of caffeine in his system.

A woman he didn't recognize sat down across from him.

"Hi," she said, smiling. "Remember me?"

"Ummmm…"

"Surely you haven't forgotten me already."

"You've got the wrong person," he said. "If we'd had any kind of meaningful interaction, I promise that I'd remember somebody like you."

She leaned across the table. "Are you flirting with me?"

"Just speaking the truth." It wasn't just her looks—and she was definitely attractive. Travis had a good memory for faces, even if it was a barista or a grocery checkout clerk, and if they'd had more than a passing encounter, he would've remembered her. She definitely had the wrong guy, which was a little disappointing. His relationship with Renee wasn't going anywhere, and she'd been ghosting him for the past several days, so he was very much available.

"I notice you're not wearing a wedding ring," she said.

"Right. It's frowned upon to wear them when you're not married."

"Girlfriend?"

"Does it count if she hasn't responded to your texts since last weekend?"

"Nope. Sure doesn't."

"Then no."

The woman held up her left hand. "What do you see here?"

"An imprint of a wedding ring."

"That's right. It came off this morning. I am free, free, free. And so, full disclosure, we've never actually met before. It was just a way for me to sit at your table without you shooing me off right away. You're by far the most appealing guy in this café."

"Thanks," said Travis. "I'm honored."

"I'm Veronica."

"Travis."

"I would never commit adultery. Never. Not ever. Not even if he cheated on me first—which he did—and not even when it took a year for our divorce to become final. That was a long, lonely year. I've been counting down the days until my court date. Guess what day that was?"

"Today?"

"First thing this morning. Now, don't misunderstand me. I'm not looking to jump the bones of every hot guy I meet. But I can celebrate with *one*, right? Doesn't that sound reasonable?"

"It sounds very reasonable."

"What's on your agenda for today?"

"Nothing I can't cancel."

"Do you have to go into work?"

"Not for a couple of hours."

"What if I wanted more than a couple of hours of your time?"

"I'm the manager. I'll let one of my employees know that I'll be late."

"You should do that."

Travis sent a quick text to Marco, the head chef. Marco responded right away, saying that it was no problem.

"We're all set," he said.

"That was easy."

"It's good to be the boss."

"Would you like to get out of here, or would you like to finish your coffee first?"

"It's already in a to-go cup. I don't live that far from here, and I don't have roommates or anything."

"House or apartment?"

"Apartment."

"Let's go to my house. Like I said, it's been a really long time. I expect to be loud."

Travis lay naked on his back, hands on Veronica's fantastic breasts. She wasn't kidding about the noise level. She was riding him like she was trying to crush him into the mattress. He had several bite marks on his chest and shoulders, and he didn't think they'd fade right away.

Nothing like this had ever happened to him before. This was like something out of a porno flick. Travis masturbated a lot on any given day—though never at work, of course—and this would have a place of honor when it was time to conjure up memories.

He'd been doing a remarkable job, endurance-wise. Once the clothes started coming off he'd been a little nervous about that, because she was horny and aggressive and he kind of got the sense that if he came before she was satisfied, she might cut his dick off. But keeping himself away from the brink hadn't been an issue, and unless she was faking it, she'd already come several times.

She leaned down and kissed him on the mouth. "I'm getting a cramp in my leg," she informed him.

"Want me to finish?"

"Yes, please."

That was all the invitation he needed. A few seconds

later he climaxed with a loud moan. Veronica climbed off him and got off the bed. "Gonna walk it off," she said. "I'll get us some drinks. You can clean up for round two."

Vivian did not feel guilty about having sex with Travis. She had enjoyed every second of it. He was bigger than Ken, his penis wasn't crooked, and he was more attentive, although that last part could be attributed to this being the first time he'd seen her naked. On the "deceiving one's spouse" scorecard, Ken was still far ahead.

She walked into the kitchen. A steak knife was fine for wedging underneath fingernails, but for this she wanted to go with the classic psychotic stabbing utensil: a butcher knife. She'd brought her own.

That's what she'd used on her three previous men, so long ago, before she decided to give it up. Had their bodies ever been found, she might have considered using a different weapon, but since they hadn't, why not use what felt good in her hand?

She heard water running in the bathroom. Vivian quickly went into the bedroom and hid the knife under her pillow. Then she returned to the kitchen and opened the refrigerator, unsure if she'd find anything in there. A six-pack of beer with four cans left, and a couple of bottles of water. She took one of the bottles and returned to the bedroom.

Veronica was sprawled out on the bed when Travis returned, looking as if she were already set for another round. He hoped she didn't think it was going to happen this soon.

She sat up and tossed him a bottle of water. "You look dehydrated."

"Not that extreme, but I'm definitely thirsty." He unscrewed the cap and downed half of the contents of the bottle, then set it on the nightstand.

She patted the bed next to her. "C'mon. You're duty-bound to snuggle me."

"I can do that." He climbed onto the bed as Veronica rolled onto her side.

"I want to spoon you," she said.

"I should be the big spoon."

"It's my divorce celebration, so I'll decide who gets to be the big spoon and who gets to be the little one. C'mon. I want to run my fingers over those six-pack abs."

"Yeah, they're under that layer of fat somewhere."

Travis rolled onto his side and Veronica pressed herself against him. She gently ran her fingers down his chest, past his navel, and down to his penis.

"You're gonna have to give me some recovery time."

"I wasn't asking you to use it again," she said, stroking him. "Just enjoying how it feels."

"As long as you're managing expectations."

"I assure you, I'm not expecting a cyborg."

They lay there for a couple of minutes. This was nice. He liked the feel of her breasts against his back, and her lips gently kissing his shoulder. He could almost fall asleep.

Veronica shifted, adjusting her pillow.

"Roll on your stomach," she told him.

"Why?"

"So I can give you a backrub."

"No funny business back there."

"Not on our first date."

Travis laughed and obliged.

She ran her hands over his back. He flinched.

"What's wrong?"

"Tickles."

"Oh, sorry."

She ran her hands over him some more. Then she switched to one hand for a while.

It felt great, but Travis was slightly worried about what she was planning to do with that other hand. He supposed she'd give him *some* warning.

"Would you still be attracted to me if I did something bad?" Veronica asked.

"Like what?" asked Travis, clenching a bit.

"Stabbed you in the back with a butcher knife."

"Excuse me?"

"Is that a no?"

Travis turned his head to look at her. "I know you're kidding, but that's still pretty—"

She shoved the pillow against his face, then slammed the knife deep into his back.

Vivian plunged the knife into his flesh, over and over.

Blood sprayed everywhere. She couldn't let him scream too loudly since it was only the basement that was soundproofed, so she stabbed him in the back of the neck a few times. After that, he was still struggling a bit, but only making a gurgling sound.

She rolled him onto his back and slashed his throat.

Let out an involuntary giggle.

Stabbed him a few more times.

She rubbed some of his blood on her breasts. Later it would be sticky and uncomfortable, but now it was warm and smooth, like chocolate syrup.

Travis wasn't moving anymore. That didn't mean she needed to quit stabbing him.

She stabbed him until her arm was sore. Then she gulped down the rest of his bottle of water and lay there for a while, catching her breath. She ran her fingers through his wet hair. He seemed like a nice guy and he was certainly a good lay, but, hey, tough shit.

She rolled him over, a task made more difficult because her hands kept slipping, and then she stabbed him some more.

This was going to take a while to clean up. She should've been more cautious. Screwed him and then lured him down into the basement.

But that wasn't her style.

Anyway, at this point the mess couldn't get much worse, so she continued to stab him until her arm just wouldn't move anymore. Her left arm wasn't tired, but stabbing with that hand was awkward and unsatisfying.

She left the butcher knife imbedded in his back and slid off the bed.

She walked into the bathroom and stared at herself in the mirror.

Vivian liked what she saw. She looked good drenched in gore.

She smiled at her reflection. Batted her bloody eyelids.

After a couple of minutes, she returned to the bedroom. She was dripping all over the carpet, but it wasn't as if she was going to wander around the entire house. As long as she remembered the path she took, she wouldn't miss any bloodstains on the floor.

God, she'd missed this.

Vivian climbed back onto the bed with Travis' body. She didn't go so far as to wrap her arm around him and cuddle, but she lay close to him, enjoying the squishy wetness of the sheets underneath her. She was in no hurry to leave. She'd have to start cleaning up soon—there was a lot of work to do if she wanted to finish before Ken got off work—but for now she simply wanted to bask in the afterglow.

She sat up, startled.

She hadn't fallen asleep, but she'd lost track of time. The blood was no longer warm.

Somebody had come in the front door. More than one person. A man and a woman. They were laughing, so it wasn't the cops. It had to be Ken's perverted buddy. Darrell?

Well, she couldn't exactly clean up this blood-splattered room before they saw it, or even get dressed. She'd have to make use of the fact that seeing a completely naked woman drenched in blood would be somewhat distracting.

She picked up the butcher knife and slid off the bed. "Help me," she said, loud enough to be heard but not shouting. She wanted them to think she'd been injured, that she was weak. She put the hand with the butcher knife behind her back and pushed out her bloody chest.

"What the hell?" the man, probably Darrell, said. She heard his footsteps as he hurriedly walked toward the bedroom.

He stepped into the doorway and gaped at the grisly sight.

Darrell was certainly no Christian Grey. He might have some extra cash but he was a grotesque male specimen, overweight and ruddy-faced. She couldn't imagine what kind of woman would willingly get his secretions on her.

The blood, the mutilated corpse, and her naked body seemed to put him into sensory overload. In a few seconds he might have wondered why her hand was behind her back, but she didn't give him a few seconds to think about it. She slammed the butcher knife into his throat, then wrenched it out to the left, opening up half of his neck. Vivian pushed past him before his body began to fall.

The horrified looking woman in the hallway was too young and pretty to be with a repulsive human being like Darrell unless there was a sugar daddy thing happening. Or maybe she was a hooker. So while she obviously didn't deserve to die, Vivian didn't feel *too* sorry for her.

Vivian didn't think she could get to her before she screamed once, but she could certainly keep her from screaming twice.

Surprisingly, the woman didn't scream. She gasped and spun around to run.

She didn't get far. Vivian stabbed her in the back, then shoved her to the floor. The woman landed hard, right on her face. If the floor weren't carpeted she might have shattered her jaw.

Vivian climbed on top of her then stabbed her in the

back of the neck, over and over, until she stopped moving. That didn't take very long.

She returned to the bedroom to make sure Darrell was dead. He was.

Vivian sat on the bed and let out a happy, satisfied sigh. She definitely should not have done this. Now she had a lot of tracks to cover, and a lot of explaining to do to Ken. The regret would hit her—it always had in the distant past—but for now she was going to enjoy a few more minutes of bliss.

CHAPTER FOURTEEN

Hi, Warren!

So upon some reflection, I've decided that it's silly to pass up this opportunity. I've had problems coping with what happened, but maybe that's exactly WHY I should tell my story. (Yes, it helps that Gertie texted me from the restaurant to let me know that you're legitimate!)

If you haven't moved on to another "hero," I'd love to get together to discuss this. Anytime today works great for me! Just let me know. Thanks!

Charlene

Ken checked to be sure nobody was walking near his cubicle, then read the e-mail on his burner phone. It was almost definitely a trap. No way in hell would he meet with her, but if he chose a public place and kept her waiting, he might be able to watch and figure out if she was working with the cops or if she was going it alone.

He didn't want the meeting to happen too soon. His no-show could confirm what she (and the cops?)

probably already suspected. He'd stretch it out until tomorrow.

Hey, Charlene, great to hear from you, and I'm glad you've changed your mind! Unfortunately, today's schedule is packed, but I can free up some time for you tomorrow morning. Breakfast?

"He wants to do breakfast," Charlene said.

After a fitful night of sleep, she'd decided that she *wasn't* being paranoid and gone to the cops. Gertie was over eighteen and hadn't been out of contact for more than twenty-four hours, but given the circumstances, the police were more than willing to call her a missing person.

They'd already done some preliminary questioning of all of the Shellfish Grotto employees who'd been there last night. Only two male servers had been working, and neither of them admitted to taking Gertie home. There was alibi-checking left to do, but any scenario involving Gertie being seduced by a server who just happened to be responsible for her missing cousin was a stretch.

The police were also questioning her other friends and family to find out if anybody had seen her since she left the restaurant. But the obvious suspect was Warren the friendly web series producer. Their server remembered Gertie and the guy she was with—glasses, great big beard, bandage on his neck—but hadn't noticed anything unusual about their interaction. She believed they left the restaurant at the same time but hadn't been paying that much attention. There were no security cameras in the parking lot.

Charlene hadn't asked Warren any questions about Gertie. They didn't want to tip him off that they suspected anything was wrong. There'd been some debate over whether to e-mail him or not, but they'd decided that the possibility of him showing up for a meeting was worth the risk of making him suspicious.

Bradley Lugens walked over to look at her laptop screen. Charlene wished she was in a room full of FBI agents working furiously to track down every lead, but it was just her and Detective Lugens, in a conference room at the police station.

"Should I push for something sooner?" Charlene asked.

"No," said Lugens. "You were pretty adamant that you weren't interested. If you go too far in the other direction, he'll know something's up. Just say yes. Let him suggest the time and the meeting spot."

Breakfast sounds great, she typed. *Give me a time/place and I'll be there! Thanks!*

After Lugens approved her message, she sent it off.

"You have to be at work at 10:45, you said?" Lugens asked.

"Yes. My boss will give me the day off if I need it."

"No, stick to your regular schedule as much as possible. Don't leave the restaurant. Do they make you carry trash outside?"

Charlene shook her head. "The dishwashers take stuff to the Dumpster."

"Okay, good. Don't go out for smoke breaks or anything like that."

"I don't smoke."

"Perfect. No fresh air or sunshine for you today. I'll drop you off and pick you up. We'll evaluate where things are tonight, but with your permission you may have a cop crashing on your sofa tonight."

"That would be wonderful. Thank you."

"I wish we could do more," said Lugens. "We don't have the resources to give you full-time protection, but we'll keep you safe, I promise."

Lugens drove her to work in an unmarked car, reminded her again not to leave the restaurant for any reason, and told her to give him a call when she was done with her shift.

During the drive, she'd made the mistake of asking him if he thought Gertie was still alive. He asked if she wanted him to be completely honest. She'd hesitated, thinking it might be nice to live in a fantasy world for a bit longer, then said yes.

"There's still a good chance that she did indeed willingly go home with somebody," he said. "The married waiter, maybe. Or somebody she didn't want to admit to you. That's our perfect scenario. But if these disappearances are indeed the work of one guy, and he's got your friend...well, that's not good news."

Charlene went inside and punched in. The restaurant opened in fifteen minutes, so right now everybody was just doing prep work. She walked over to the chef's station, where Marco was busy dicing green peppers.

"Where's Travis?" she asked.

"Gonna be late. Got errands to run."

"He's coming in late because he needs to run errands?"

"That's what he said."

"That doesn't sound like him. Did he say what he was doing?"

"Nope," said Marco. "I didn't ask. Not in the habit of interrogating my boss."

"Okay, thanks." Charlene returned to the back room, took out her cell phone, and gave Travis a call. It went straight to voice mail.

She typed in a text: *Hey, call me ASAP, okay? Gertie's gone missing.*

No, wait. Charlene was probably far overreaching the scope of the problem, but if Travis *was* in danger, the culprit might have access to his phone. She deleted the message and retyped it.

Hey, give me a call when you get a chance. Might need to come in late tomorrow.

She sent it off, hoping there'd be an immediate response, and then she could call him to hear his voice.

No response.

No reason to freak out yet, but she did call Lugens to let him know.

The day was maddening. Charlene wanted to do something to help, yet there was nothing she could do on her own that wouldn't put Gertie (and Travis?) at more risk. She absolutely would not ignore Lugens' orders about staying in the restaurant. That would be stupid. Which meant that all she could do was wait tables and helplessly hope that Gertie or Travis would return her message.

Neither of them returned her message.

She tried to think of some clue she could've missed, but the situation seemed pretty straightforward: Gertie had gone to dinner with "Warren," and he kidnapped her. The mystery was whether she was still alive.

Charlene believed that she was.

She also believed that she might be deluding herself.

Though she didn't dump lasagna on anybody, she didn't provide very good customer service for the first few hours of her shift, and her tips suffered accordingly. She also had to go into the walk-in freezer, shut the door, press her apron against her mouth, and muffle a frustrated scream.

Everything hurt.

Gertie's fingers hurt the worst, of course, followed by her stabbed legs. The rest of her body was in agony from having so little room to move in the cage. She couldn't imagine what it would be like if she wasn't so thin. Plus she had a pounding headache and was sick to her stomach.

She wasn't ready to die, though.

Her body was in terrible shape, but she had a lot of fight left in her. If Ken or Vivian got too close and dropped their guard for just a second, she'd tear their face off with her teeth. She was not going to die in this goddamn cage.

Though she was at a loss for how to avoid dying in the cage.

Swinging it hadn't worked. She'd hoped that it would eventually pop free of the ceiling, but it never happened and eventually she was too exhausted to continue. Bouncing around in the cage—not that she had much room to do so—hadn't worked either. Her captivity was not a flimsy setup.

She'd screamed for help for a while, but of course nobody came to investigate, and she was only hurting her throat.

Since screaming and swinging didn't work, that left her options to escape as...none.

Nothing unless Ken or Vivian discovered the kindness in their hearts.

Or got too close.

Vivian's car wasn't in the driveway when Ken got home. He went inside and upstairs to Jared's room. His son, not so shockingly, was staring at a video game in progress.

"Where's your mom?" Ken asked.

Jared shrugged.

"You wanna pause that and acknowledge me?"

Jared paused the game. "I said I don't know where she is."

"She didn't text you or anything?"

"She left a note on the table."

"What did it say?"

"Something like *Went out. Be back soon.*"

"So you could have started there instead of pretending like you didn't know what I was talking about."

"You asked if I knew where she was," Jared said.

Ken decided that continuing this conversation would lead to mental illness. He was very interested in Vivian's whereabouts, so he wasn't sure if he wanted to waste time by pointing out the faint marijuana scent or not. But he didn't want Jared to think that he was oblivious. "Can you at least try to hide the pot smell, instead of assuming that I won't notice?"

"I wasn't smoking pot," said Jared. "I just say no to drugs."

"Okay, smartass, then why does your room smell like weed?"

Jared shrugged.

"Let me answer that for you. It smells like weed because you were smoking a joint in here before I got home, and then you did a bad job of getting rid of the smell because you're either lazy or figured I wouldn't give a shit."

"If I was smoking weed, how come I'm not stoned?"

"How do I know you're not stoned right now? You think you're being such a brilliant conversationalist that there's no way you could be high?"

"Ask me to count backwards or something."

Ken sighed and left the room. He'd search it later. He hated to admit such a thing about his own offspring, but Jared was probably dumb enough to leave evidence in his room even after this conversation.

He went downstairs and texted Vivian to ask where she was. She texted back and said she was at the house.

No, you're not. I'm at the house.

You know which house I mean. Come over.

Why the hell was she at the other house? Ken cursed under his breath and called out to Jared: "Hey, I'm heading out for a while! You're on your own for dinner!"

"Can I have money for pizza?" Jared called down.

"No. There are leftovers in the fridge."

Jared didn't say anything, at least not that Ken could hear. Ken left the house and went back to his car. He called Vivian as he started the engine.

"Hi," she said, quietly.

"Why are you over there?"

"We should talk in person." Her voice was a monotone.

"Give me a hint."

A moment of silence. "We should talk in person."

"Am I going to be unhappy?"

"You're wasting time. Just come over here."

"No, I'm not wasting time. My talking doesn't make the car move slower. I'd like some sort of idea of what's going on."

She hung up on him.

Ken didn't call her back. If she'd decided that she wasn't going to explain anything over the phone, no amount of screaming at her would change her mind. He'd find out what happened when he got there. He didn't *know* it was bad. Maybe he'd arrive and find Charlene in the living room, gift wrapped and ready to be caged.

He tried to focus on that possibility as he drove, rather than the possibility that she'd done something horrible.

He arrived at the house twenty minutes later. Vivian was seated on the couch, hands in her lap, her face blank. This was definitely not a "Hey, I've got a present for you!" scenario. He closed the front door and waited for her to speak. When he realized that she wasn't going to speak without prompting, he asked her what was going on.

Vivian patted the couch cushion next to her. Ken sat down.

"You're creeping me out," he said.

Vivian took a deep breath. "I did something I regret."

"I kind of figured that. What did you do?"

"You have to promise me you won't get mad."

"No."

"It's not as bad as what you did."

"For fuck's sake, Vivian, just tell me what you did! Did you kill Gertie?"

Vivian shook her head.

"So talk! Spit it out! You're driving me insane!"

"Now I'm not sure you're ready to handle it."

Ken stood up and resisted the urge to kick the couch. He stormed out of the living room and walked into the hallway. He entered two digits of the code to open the basement door before he noticed the smell of ammonia. The carpet was damp.

He went into Darrell's bedroom. The smell of cleaning supplies was even thicker in here. In addition to the damp carpet, the bed had been completely stripped of sheets and blankets, and the mattress itself was wet, as if it had been scrubbed down.

Things were getting further and further away from "gift wrapped victim."

He went back into the living room.

"Okay," he said, straining to keep his voice calm, "I swear I won't get mad. Just tell me what you did. We'll work through this together."

"You know the girl you're after? The one on the news? The one whose friend is in the basement?"

"Yes, I know who you're talking about. Her name is Charlene. Did you kill her?"

"No. I killed her boss."

"How?"

"I brought him back here and stabbed him to death."

"Did you have sex with him?"

"No. Of course not."

Ken's face felt like it was on fire. He wanted to go over there and smack the shit out of her, though of course he'd never lay a hand on her. He tried to figure out what to say, but couldn't formulate a response that wasn't simply a string of expletives, so he settled for pacing around the room for a few moments.

"This was your fault," said Vivian.

"How the hell was it my fault?"

"You betrayed my trust. And it made me want to have my fun, too."

"You couldn't have talked to me about it?"

"You didn't talk to me."

"Actually, I did."

"No, you withheld the worst parts. You told me the women were already dead. You didn't tell me about the depraved stuff in the basement. You didn't tell me about this place. Don't you dare pretend that you were honest with me."

Ken continued to pace. "Fine. Fine. You murdered her boss. Should I expect the cops to break down this door at any minute?"

"Of course not. I was careful."

"How careful? You're twenty years out of practice."

"Nobody knows."

"All right. Shit. How far did it go?"

"What do you mean? I told you I stabbed him to death. That's pretty fucking far."

"You stabbed him to death on the bed. How far did it go? Were you rolling around naked? Did you go down on him? Did you make out? What happened?"

"He thought he was going to get laid, obviously," said Vivian, "but nothing happened. I told him I was going to give him a backrub to relax him. All he got was a knife."

Ken wasn't entirely convinced that Vivian was telling the truth, though she wasn't avoiding eye contact or fidgeting or giving off any of the other nonverbal clues that somebody was lying. If she'd kissed the guy to lure him onto the bed...well, he wouldn't think about that.

"I wish you hadn't done this," Ken told her.

"So do I," Vivian admitted.

Ken sighed. "Well, what's done is done, I guess. We obviously can't bring him back to life. We'll just have to make sure we've covered your tracks completely."

"I covered them," said Vivian. "Nobody will ever find out."

"All right. Is there anything else I should know?"

CHAPTER FIFTEEN

Vivian did not answer right away.

In fact, now she was avoiding eye contact.

Ken was not happy about this. "What happened?" he asked.

"There were complications."

"What kind of complications?"

"You swore you wouldn't get mad."

"Right. I'll stick to that. Just tell me about these complications."

"Your gross friend showed up with a gross woman and I had no other choice."

Ken suddenly felt like he needed the flask of whiskey that he kept in the glove compartment. His legs went numb and for a moment he thought he might keel over right there. "Had no other choice but to do what?"

"What do you think? You can't put the pieces together?"

"Please tell me you're just messing with me."

"You're the one who rented a house with a sleaze bucket. I'm sorry I had to do it, but it's not like the world has lost a fine human being. He was a sweaty pig who brought some slut over for a lunchtime fuck session. Boo-hoo. Society will cope."

"I'm not saying that he was an upstanding citizen. I don't give a shit that he's dead. I give a shit that you murdered three people in a day! I chose my victims carefully. I spaced them out. You went on a killing spree!"

"What was I supposed to do? Tell them to ignore all of the gore; the maid would take care of it?"

"Make up an excuse! Send them away! Tell him that you found out I was renting the place and you were pissed!"

"I was covered in blood. I can't help but think they might have suspected that something was amiss."

"He's got a wife!"

"So? I'm guessing that he didn't tell her where he was going or who he was with. He was here to bang his mistress. He covered his own tracks."

Ken couldn't believe they were having this conversation. It was difficult for him to not just start smashing his head against the wall until his skull shattered. This was absolute madness.

"Shit," he said. "Shit, shit, shit."

"Why are you so upset?"

"You knew I'd done this kind of thing before."

"Yeah, and you said you'd gotten it out of your system before we met."

"Well, apparently you brought it right back. I thought you might be happy. This opens the door to us doing it together."

"You seriously thought I'd say, 'Good job, honey!' For real?"

"No," said Vivian. "But maybe we could discuss the

idea that this isn't necessarily such a bad thing."

"It *is* a bad thing. You better have gotten it out of your system this time, because you're done! It's over. Where are the bodies?"

"In the trunk of my car."

"How'd you get them in there by yourself?"

"I made them easier to carry."

"Jesus."

"There were tools in the garage."

"And where exactly did you plan to get rid of them?" Ken asked.

"I don't know. You're the one with corpses in cages. Where did you plan to get rid of yours?"

"I was going to bury them in the forest."

"Good. That's what we'll do with mine."

Ken was feeling a bit dizzy. "I need to sit down," he said, plopping down on the couch.

Vivian scooted closer to him. "Maybe this gives us a reason to get out of here. Leave and start over. You hate your job. We've got some savings."

"What about Jared's school?"

"So he does his senior year at a new school. It's not like he's leaving behind many friends. It might be better for him to be someplace where nobody knows about the cat."

"I'm sure nobody remembers the cat."

"Would you forget if it was one of your classmates? He's lucky they thought it only happened once. What I'm saying is that he'll be fine. We could move him to the North Pole and he wouldn't care as long as he had his video games."

"We can't just—"

"I know what you're going to say," said Vivian.

"Obviously we aren't going to pack up and leave right after these people have gone missing. We'll wait it out a little bit. But not too long. Go somewhere with a really cheap cost of living."

"You mean where life is cheap?"

Vivian shrugged. "Maybe."

"I don't kill crack whores or homeless people."

"That's not what I was saying at all. You need to chill out."

"Chill out? After what you did?"

"We'd already agreed that I got to do it."

"No!" Ken vigorously shook his head. "We absolutely did not agree on that. You said you got to kill somebody, but we did not come to any kind of decision. I never would have allowed that. Never."

"My mistake."

"It's great that you can be oh-so-very casual about this. Sorry if I'm not feeling quite as safe."

Vivian got up off the couch. "What you did is worse. Despite that, we're going to call it even. Starting right now, what you did doesn't matter and what I did doesn't matter."

"Of course it fucking matters!"

"I meant in terms of our relationship. Yes, we have work to do, but you got your women in cages, I got my victim and the collateral damage, and we're done fighting about it."

"I don't know that I am."

"I'll give you another one. The other girl. Charlene."

"What the hell are you saying? She's here?"

"No, no, no. Nothing like that. I'm just giving you permission to go after her."

"For real?"

"Yes. And by that, the message I'm sending is that I trust you to be careful. I'd like you to trust me the same way."

Ken didn't trust her, but he sure as hell wasn't going to throw away this opportunity. It still *enraged* him that Charlene was walking around free after trying to help her friend lure him out, and if he could have those girls in side-by-side cages, it might be worth the nagging feeling that Vivian had probably let their boss feel her up before she murdered him.

He gave his wife a hug. "I do trust you," he whispered into her ear.

"Thank you," she said. "I'm sorry."

"I'm sorry, too. From now on, no secrets."

"No secrets."

Ken pulled away. "I assume you didn't mean that I should go after her today, but I think there's a window of opportunity."

Hey, Charlene! My schedule just cleared a bit this evening. By any chance are you available around 8:00? If Gertie wanted to tag along, that would be fantastic—we had a great meeting yesterday, and I could give you both more information about the approach I'm going to take.

P.S.: Obviously you haven't signed on yet. No pressure!

Charlene forwarded the e-mail to Lugens and called

him.

"Tell him yes," said Lugens. "Don't say anything about Gertie. Just say yes and ask him where."

Ken gave her the address of a bar. Bad part of town. Usually crowded. It would be difficult for the police to keep tabs on the customers and look for somebody suspicious, because just about everyone in that shithole looked suspicious. Ken had gone there a couple of times, searching for potential victims, but he'd had no luck.

Of course, he wasn't going to be there, at eight o'clock or otherwise. He just wanted the cops to think they might have a place to nab him.

"We've got a couple people in there posing as customers," Lugens told Charlene over the phone. "It's a terrible place for a business meeting. We get called out there all the time."

"What time are we going to get there?"

"Early. Seven-thirty. I'll explain everything to you on the ride over, but you'll have a plainclothes cop on the barstool on each side of you. Anybody who approaches you for any reason gets discreetly steered away and questioned. Another cop will be posing as a bouncer, so he'll be checking IDs as everybody comes in. We'll also be keeping an eye on people outside the venue. Either a legitimate web series producer is going to have a very startling meeting, or we're gonna catch this guy."

"Thanks," said Charlene. "I'm looking forward to being his bait."

"Don't call it bait. We'll keep you safe. He won't get close enough to touch you."

"I really hope he shows."

"Me too. I'll be there to pick you up when your shift ends."

Ken hated his new look.

Though Vivian had declared that his short spiked bleach blonde hair looked "sexy," he thought it looked ridiculous. But he couldn't use the hipster beard disguise again, just in case any of last night's restaurant patrons had described the person Gertie had been with. He'd added some makeup to give himself a bad complexion (which Vivian did not declare to be sexy).

He spent about half an hour outside of the Italian restaurant, watching for people who seemed to be waiting in vehicles for no particular reason. The restaurant had a large parking lot and there really wasn't anywhere for somebody to keep tabs on the area while pretending to do something other than lurk outside of a restaurant. Of course, the same was true for him, but if a police officer approached his car, he'd just say that he was waiting for his dinner date, and then he'd abandon the plan. But it was pretty clear that nobody was watching the place.

Ken got out of the car. Now he had to be bold. Not suicidally bold, but bold.

He waited for a couple to walk through the front door, and followed immediately behind them. While they spoke with the hostess, he walked past them and through the restaurant.

There she was.

She was with a table of four, taking a glass from a diner who apparently wanted a refill. She didn't glance over at Ken as he walked by her. He imagined grabbing a handful of her hair, twisting it around his fingers, then slamming her head into the table, enjoying the screaming of the customers as her teeth bounced into their spaghetti.

But, of course, his plan wasn't *that* bold. He walked into the bathroom. An elderly gentleman was washing his hands. After he left, Ken checked to make sure the stall was vacant. He'd hoped the restroom would be the one-person-at-a-time model, so he could lock the door, but as long as nobody had a full bladder in the next thirty seconds he'd be fine.

He took out his burner phone and called the restaurant.

"Davey's Italian Grill," a woman answered. "How may I help you?"

"My name is Richard Goshen of the Emergency Response Team. We've received a credible bomb threat at your location. We've dispatched a bomb squad, but we need you to evacuate the restaurant immediately. Don't say it's a bomb. Call it a 'situation' so you don't cause panic. Just get everybody outside in a quick and orderly fashion and make sure they're at least five hundred feet away from the building. Do you understand?"

"Is this a joke?"

"It is *not* a joke and we have reason to believe the

culprit has every intention of detonating the device. We'll be there in less than four minutes, but you need to get everybody out of the building right away. Do you understand?"

"Yes. Yes, sir. I'll do it right now."

Ken tucked the phone back into his pocket and exited the restroom. It might have been simpler to just pull the fire alarm, but he didn't want cops to show up any sooner than necessary. The hostess stepped into the main dining area. "Ladies and gentlemen!" she said, repeating the statement three more times until the restaurant was quiet enough for her to be heard by everybody. "I'm going to need you to exit the restaurant. Everything will be explained when the police show up, but we have a situation and I need everybody to leave the building in a quick but orderly fashion."

Some of the customers looked at each other, confused. Others got up.

"This is not a drill!" said the hostess. "We need to clear out this building immediately."

Now more people got up. Others hurried for the exit.

Ken made a beeline for Charlene.

What was she supposed to do?

The idea that there was a genuine emergency at the restaurant on the same day that she'd been instructed not to leave was too much of a coincidence. Charlene couldn't just file out of the building with the rest of the customers and employees. But she had to assume that this was about her, so she had to be on high alert.

She took out her cell phone to call Lugens.

"Nope," said a blonde man, walking up next to her and speaking in a low voice. "Put the phone away or I'll shoot you in the side."

Charlene stopped walking and put the phone back in her pocket. She wished she had the sleight of hand to make the call just as she slipped the phone away, but she was no magician.

"Keep walking," he said. "Same pace as everybody else. This is the only way you'll save your friend's life."

For a moment, Charlene considered not playing along, but rather attacking him, screaming and trying to claw out his eyes with her fingernails. But she had no reason to doubt that he had a gun, and if she drew attention to him, he in turn would have no reason not to shoot her. She walked forward, trying to make desperate eye contact with somebody, but the other people in the restaurant were preoccupied with their own concerns.

They walked out of the building. Abigail the hostess shouted for everybody to move at least five hundred feet away and that the police would be here in two or three minutes.

"You fuck around with me, you die," the man informed Charlene. "And then Gertie dies really badly. I mean, *really* badly."

"How do I know she's even still alive?"

"Oh, I'll show you. I'll put your mind at ease, don't worry. Have you been in touch with the cops?"

"No."

"That's a lie. Don't lie to me. Give me your phone."

She took out her phone again and the man snatched it out of her hand. He led her to his automobile and opened the passenger door. "Get in," he said, giving her a gentle shove. She got in, frantically looking around for something she could use as a weapon.

The man hurried around to the driver's side. He opened the door, knelt down, then got inside the car, no longer holding her phone. He shut the door and turned on the engine.

"Behave and you won't get hurt," he said. "This can end horribly for both of us, or we can both play it cool."

"Show me the proof that Gertie's alive."

"When we're in the clear." He reached under his shirt and took a revolver out of the waistline of his jeans. "Just in case you thought I was bluffing. I don't want to use this, so don't make me."

He backed out of the parking space. As they drove away, Charlene saw her phone on the pavement, where the front tire had rolled over it.

"Somebody's gonna find my phone," she told him.

The man shrugged. "I don't care if they find it there. I just don't want them tracing it."

"So you're Warren?"

"Ken, actually."

Charlene really, really didn't like that he'd told her his real name. She wished she hadn't asked in the first place. Maybe he was lying. Maybe Ken wasn't his name. God, she hoped it wasn't.

"You're a pretty selfless girl," said Ken. "I saw that on the news. Offering to be that psychopath's hostage and stuff. Well, we're going to have to tap into that, because you may get scared and try to escape. If you try—even if you don't succeed, which you won't—Gertie will die. And I mean *die*. Keep that in mind."

"I'm not going to try to escape," Charlene assured him. She could no longer see the restaurant in the rearview mirror.

"Good girl," said Ken. "Keep making this easy."

Ken drove down the street, sticking to the speed limit. He was in the right-hand lane, so when he stopped at a red light, there were no adjacent drivers for Charlene to signal to. She wouldn't do anything with her hands, but a mouthed "*Call the police!*" might send the message without him noticing.

The revolver was in his lap. He was mostly steering with his right hand, but even when he had both hands on the wheel, she didn't see any way she could grab the weapon. A sudden attack would probably just end with her being gut-shot...though she would keep watching for an opportunity.

"Hypothetical question for you," said Ken.

"Okay."

"Do you know what color nail polish Gertie wears?"

"No."

"You sure? Think hard."

Charlene wanted to throw up. This line of questioning could not be headed anywhere good. "I really don't know."

"Are her nails short or long?"

"Short, I think. Long nails aren't good when you're carrying trays all day."

"But the color. You have no idea?"

"Maybe turquoise."

"*Maybe* turquoise? Or definitely turquoise?"

"Definitely."

Ken nodded. "Thanks. I guess my wife was right. Figures."

"I don't understand what I'm supposed to be getting out of this conversation."

"My wife wanted to cut off Gertie's finger and give it to you as proof that we had her. My concern was that you wouldn't recognize the finger as belonging to Gertie. Obviously, the severed finger would upset you, but if you can't identify who it came from, what's the point? But apparently you *would* have known it was Gertie's, so she still has ten fingers for nothing."

"Oh," said Charlene, having nothing else to contribute.

"Instead, I made a video. Truthfully, I don't need to show it to you—I mean, you're already in the car. I made it in case my plan didn't go smoothly and you needed extra persuasion. But I said I'd prove that she was alive, and it would be a dick move to go back on that. Open the glove compartment."

Charlene did not reach for the glove compartment.

"It's not a trick," said Ken. "Her finger isn't in there. It's a phone."

"I don't need to see the video," said Charlene.

Ken shrugged. "Your choice."

They drove for a couple more minutes, during which time Charlene debated whether or not she should open the glove compartment. She didn't want to pop it open and have ten severed fingers spill out onto her lap. On the other hand, she should be acquiring as much information as possible. If there *was* a video from Gertie, it would show where she was. Or at least where she'd been when Ken made the recording.

She opened the glove compartment.

It was empty except for a cell phone.

"It's the only video on there," Ken told her. "Don't forget that I've got the gun. I promise, you won't make it through all three digits of 911."

Charlene believed that she could indeed dial the entirety of 911 before he put a bullet in her skull, but he'd kill her before she could finish her conversation with the dispatcher. So she followed instructions and played the video.

It was a close-up of Gertie's face, looking terrified. There was a smear of blood on her cheek.

"What do you have to say to Charlene?" an unseen Ken asked.

"Don't come after me! He's going to kill you! Just stay—"

The video ended.

"Sorry, she went off-message and I had to cut it short," said Ken. "Put the phone back in the glove compartment and close it."

Charlene did as she was told. For a fraction of a second she considered abandoning caution and just grabbing for his gun, or jerking the steering wheel to send the car careening into a crosswalk signal, but she didn't think that would work out well for her or Gertie.

"She's wrong," said Ken. "I'm not going to kill you."

"Okay."

"I'm going to lock you in a cage and watch you starve to death. It won't be me killing you. It'll be biology."

Charlene said nothing.

"You're not going to try to change my mind?" Ken asked.

"Would it work?"

"No. I'm just surprised. This is a refreshing change. Usually there's a lot of begging and pleading. They tell me about their kids. Offer sexual favors."

"I'd rather starve to death in a cage than touch your dick."

Charlene assumed he'd respond with something like a sadistic chuckle, but he looked genuinely angry. He was silent for a moment. "Bitch," he finally said.

She decided not to taunt him for his pathetic retort. Instead, she asked, "If I'm going to die anyway, why shouldn't I go for the gun?"

"Because you think you still have a chance of saving your friend and yourself. If you make me shoot you, that possibility goes away. You spend your last moments trying to plug the holes that are spurting blood."

Charlene couldn't deny that Ken's words were a good deterrent. He didn't seem like a criminal mastermind. He'd mess up.

A couple of minutes later, he pulled into the parking lot of a convenience store with boards over the windows. He drove behind the building, put the car into park, and pointed the gun at Charlene's face.

"I'm going to chloroform you now," he informed her. "Are you going to make this easy for me, or hard?"

"I'm probably going to make it hard," said Charlene.

And she did. But in the end, everything went black.

CHAPTER SIXTEEN

The deep scratch that went from Ken's wrist to his elbow hurt like hell, but at least Charlene hadn't gotten his face. Charlene's face had not been so lucky, though the nasty bruise was the least of her upcoming worries.

After the garage door of the rental house closed, Ken opened the passenger-side door. Charlene was unconscious and wouldn't be waking up anytime soon without smelling salts, but for some reason he felt uneasy leaving her alone, even if it was just long enough to go inside and tell Vivian that his plan had worked. Instead, he not so gently lifted Charlene out of the car and awkwardly carried her inside.

Vivian was seated on the living room couch. "Nice work," she said.

"Thanks."

"She's cute."

"I didn't touch her."

"I didn't say you touched her. I just said that she was cute. I wasn't accusing you of anything."

Vivian stood up as Ken set Charlene on the couch. "It

worked great. No complications. I mean, she fought back when I knocked her out, but nothing happened that we need to worry about."

"That's good," said Vivian.

"What's wrong?" Ken asked.

"Nothing's wrong."

"You're acting weird."

"You just carried in an unconscious girl that you're going to murder. I'm not going to act completely normal."

Ken stared at her. "You stabbed three people to death a few hours ago. So tell me what's going on."

"I said we could do this as a team."

"Right. And I said no. I'm not into that idea at all. At all."

"It might bring us closer together."

"It's not up for discussion. I'm taking her down to the basement and putting her in her cage. End of talk. We're done."

"We're not done," said Vivian. "Maybe you don't think we should do this as a couple. Fine. But we're a family and we should behave that way."

"What are you getting at?"

"What do you think I'm getting at?"

"You tell me, since I really don't like what I'm hearing."

"Our family has problems. We all know it. You and I bicker all the time, Jared barely talks to us, he gets in trouble at school—maybe he needs an outlet."

"He has an outlet. You think he's just playing Mario Kart with the girls who come over?"

"I know what he's doing with those girls. I'm not as oblivious as you think I am. I know about your talk, where you told him he'd be on his own if he got one of them pregnant. Going for father of the year, huh?"

"Were you spying on us?"

Vivian let out an incredulous laugh. "No, I wasn't spying on you! I wasn't even home! He told me about it. Jared trusts me. We have no secrets. I drove one of the girls out of town to get an abortion."

"I'm sorry, *what?*"

"You heard me. It was months ago. Her parents paid for it. Jared was very supportive of her."

"Fine," said Ken. "He was nice to some chick he knocked up. What does this have to do with us coming together as a family?"

"You're not listening."

"Apparently not."

"Do you think Jared didn't know about you?"

"I beg your fucking pardon?"

"He didn't know you were a psychopath who locked women in cages, but he knew about your cover story. He's known about it since your first victim."

Ken's mind was reeling. Surely she was making all of this up. Vivian just wanted to inflict psychological torture on him. She was insane.

"If Jared is in this house, I'll..." Ken trailed off.

"You'll what?" Vivian asked.

"I don't know."

"You'll hit me? Strangle me? Lock me in a cage?"

"Is Jared here?"

Vivian nodded. "He's downstairs."

Ken wanted to scream "*Are you out of your mind?*" at her, but only the basement was soundproofed. She had to be messing with him. This couldn't possibly be real. No way would she bring their son to this house.

"Please tell me you're lying," he said.

"I'm not."

"So you told him what you did?"

"I spared him some of the details, but yes."

"You told our son, our sixteen-year-old son, that you committed three murders today? One of them completely planned and in cold blood?" Ken couldn't believe he was asking this question.

"Yes."

"Oh my God."

"He knew about the men I killed before he was born."

"How long has he known?"

"A while."

"How the hell was I kept in the dark about this?"

"I suppose you were too focused on your own playthings."

Ken plopped down on the couch next to Charlene. Yesterday things had been so simple. Now everything was spiraling out of control. He just sat there, massaging his forehead to make the sudden splitting headache go away. He had one obvious question, and assumed that Vivian would offer the answer without prompting, but she simply watched him.

"What did Jared say when you told him?" he asked.

"He was happy."

"He was happy?"

"As happy as Jared gets, yes."

"Okay, but what the hell did he *say*?"

"He is literally fifteen seconds away from you. Why are you interrogating me instead of just going down there and talking to him?"

"Because I'd like some sort of clue about what I'm in for."

"I told you he was happy."

"That's not enough information."

"He was completely into the idea of the family kill."

"What?"

"Are you going to keep asking me to repeat myself, or are you going to go downstairs and talk to your son?"

"A family kill was never on the table," said Ken. "That wasn't the deal. That was never the deal. She's mine."

"I thought you could show him how it's done."

"How it's done is I put her in a cage and watch. That's it. It's not a shared family experience."

"Well, maybe you could do this one a little differently."

"No! Why didn't you tell me any of this before I went after her? In what universe should I come home and find out that you went behind my back and invited our goddamn son to kill a woman with me? You're supposed to be the rational one in the household! Do you have any concept of how fucked up this conversation is? Any concept at all?"

"I do, actually," said Vivian. "And I'm the one with our best interests in mind. It's all out in the open now. No secrets."

"No secrets. Great." Ken stood up, causing Charlene's unconscious body to flop over onto its side. "Why stop here? How about the next time we decide to have sex, we invite Jared into the bedroom to watch? Huh? How about that?"

"Don't be disgusting."

"I don't think you get that if people had to decide which was more mentally ill, a teenage boy watching his parents fuck, or Mom, Dad, and Junior killing somebody together, almost everybody would choose the murder."

"I suppose you took a survey on your way over?"

"Listen to me," said Ken. "However you think this is going to play out, you're wrong. We're not going to become the goddamn family that slays together."

"How long are we going to argue about this?" Vivian pointed to Charlene. "Until she wakes up?"

"She's not going to wake up."

"She will if we don't wrap this up. We can't stand around fighting forever. It's a school night."

Ken sighed. "All right. I'll go talk to him. Shit."

The boy, Jared, just sat there, staring at Gertie.

He was tall, broad-shouldered, and handsome. He looked like he should be captain of the football team, not some creepy teenager sitting in a wooden chair watching Gertie hang in the cage.

After his mother left, Gertie had tried to reason with him. He'd told her to shut up or he'd break her neck. She'd believed him. So they sat in silence, with Jared occasionally chewing on his lip, leering at her as if she were naked. He'd been there for at least an hour.

They both looked over as the door opened.

The woman in Ken's arms had her head lolled over, so there was about one second where Gertie could pretend that it might not be Charlene. But of course it was Charlene.

Gertie hadn't wept since being left alone with Jared. Now the tears began to flow again.

"Get up," said Ken. "I need the chair."

Jared stood up. Ken placed Charlene in the chair. She slumped over, but he straightened her before she could tumble onto the floor.

Vivian walked into the room. She placed her hand over her nose and mouth as she recoiled at the scent. The smell of dead bodies hadn't seemed to bother Jared, even when he first walked into the room.

Ken looked uncomfortable. Nervous, even. He fidgeted as he stood there, looking like he was trying to work up the courage to say something to his son.

"So..." he finally said.

"It's okay, Dad," said Jared. "We don't have to talk about it."

"All right."

Jared placed his hand on Charlene's shoulder. Gertie wanted to shout a vicious threat about what she'd do to him if he harmed her friend, but of course there was absolutely nothing she could do to stop him, and she'd be better off conserving her very limited energy.

"Mom said we might kill her together," said Jared.

"We might," said Ken, sounding very unsure of this. "Do you really think you're ready for something like this?"

When Jared smiled, it was the creepiest grin Gertie had ever seen on an actual person. "Oh, yeah. For sure."

"No," said Ken. "Not 'Oh yeah, for sure.' This is serious. We're talking about taking a human life. You need to be absolutely certain that this is something you want to do. We can't have you throwing up and running out of the house to confess what you've done."

"How do you know this is my first time?" Jared asked.

"It damn well better be."

"All right, it is. But you don't need to treat me like a little kid. I'm not gonna start crying or turn into a tattletale. It's all good."

"I'm not in favor of this at all," said Ken. "Not even a little bit. But I guess I'm outvoted."

"I guess you are," said Vivian.

"How are we going to do this?"

"Pliers?" Jared suggested. "A lighter?"

Ken shook his head. "No. Nothing like that. She's going to die slowly but we're not doing any of that sadistic shit. We're not gouging out her eyeball and sticking your dick in the socket or anything like that."

"Jesus, Dad."

"I mean it."

"You think I was gonna take out my dick in front of Mom?"

"Enough, you two," said Vivian.

"No pliers," said Ken. "No lighter. No hydrochloric acid, or sandpaper, or nail gun, or anything that turns us into a pack of degenerate hillbillies."

"Knives, then?" Vivian asked.

"Yes. We'll tie her to the chair and go at her with knives. Nice and simple. But we don't have any rope."

"We do have rope," said Vivian. "We got some on the way over here."

"Okay. Jared, go get the rope."

"No, I'll get it. I need a break from the smell. I'll grab some knives, too." Vivian left the room.

Gertie heard Vivian's footsteps as she went up the stairs. When the stairs stopped creaking, Jared smirked at his father. "Wow, Dad. Chicks in cages. And you got pissed at me for getting in trouble at school."

"Is this a joke to you? Do you think this is funny?"

"I think it's kind of funny, yeah."

"Well, you'd better change that attitude really quick."

"Don't worry, I get it," said Jared. He pointed to

Gertie. "I liked watching her up there. She's scared as hell. I mean, look at her."

Gertie lowered her head. Yes, she was indeed scared as hell, but she wasn't going to just sit there and let them get pleasure from her terrified face.

"So maybe we lock the other one up there," said Ken. "You and I can come check on them whenever we want."

"Nah. I'd rather cut her."

Jared stood in place and leered at Gertie while Ken paced around the room. The creaking on the stairs resumed, and Vivian returned with a coil of rope, still with plastic wrap around it from wherever she'd purchased it, and three knives. She closed the door behind her.

Gertie and Vivian watched (Gertie helplessly, Vivian with glee) as the men tied Charlene to the chair.

Jared took the largest of the three knives from his mother. He held the knife up to Charlene's face.

"Not yet," said Ken.

"What's wrong?"

"What do you mean, what's wrong? What do you *think* is wrong?"

"I don't know."

"Is she awake yet?"

"I figured she'd wake up when I cut her."

"We don't just start hacking away. We wake her up first. Let her become aware of her surroundings. Talk to her."

Jared nodded. "That makes sense."

"So we need the smelling salts."

"Where are they?"

"Over in that corner."

Jared walked out of Gertie's line of sight for a moment, then returned with a small bottle. He handed it to Ken, who unscrewed the lid and held it underneath Charlene's nose.

Charlene jolted awake, eyes wide. She thrashed around but the ropes were too tight for her to escape. Then she screamed.

Ken put a finger to his lips. "Shhhhh. Stop it. I'll hurt you if you don't shut up."

It took a few more moments for Charlene to stop screaming. She looked up at Gertie, and then at her three captors, and Gertie had never witnessed such raw terror. Although she might have earlier, if she'd had a mirror.

"This is all on you," Ken told her. "If you'd stayed home and minded your own business, none of this would have happened. But you became a danger to me, which means I had to become a danger to you. So you're not getting out of this alive, and I'm not going to lie to you, it's going to be rough. But, hey, you get to be the catalyst for some family bonding time, so you've done your good deed for the day."

"Can we cut her now?" asked Jared.

"Yeah."

"Can I slice off her ear?"

"No. You don't go straight for the ear. Do you know how much blood comes out of a severed ear?"

"No, but neither do you if you just watch them starve to death in cages."

"I know enough to know that it bleeds a lot. Hell, I'm sure your mom has done it. She's probably the queen of severed ears. Viv, how much blood spurts out when you slice off somebody's ear?"

"A lot," said Vivian.

"There's your answer. So riddle me this: when you're trying to prolong somebody's death, do you want a lot of blood to spurt out of the side of their head?"

"All right, fine," said Jared. "I get it."

"Don't 'all right, fine' me. Answer the question sincerely."

"No. I don't want a lot of blood to spurt out of the side of their head."

"See? You're learning."

"Where should I cut her, then? Her arm?"

"Her arm is a good place to start."

"Wait, hold on," said Charlene.

"Okay, now she's about to start begging," said Ken. "Is that something you want to hear?"

Jared nodded. "Sure."

"All right, then. Listen to what she has to say. Maybe she'll make an interesting offer."

"Let Gertie go," said Charlene. "Keep me here if you want, but let her go."

"Now this is where your bullshit filter comes into play," said Ken. "Nobody is that selfless. She's trying to buy some time. She wants you to make a mistake."

Charlene frantically shook her head. "No, that's not true."

"Actually, it's very true. The logic doesn't hold up. Gertie is the one who got you into this mess in the first place, so she should be the one offering to sacrifice herself for you. The other way around doesn't make sense. Also, it's a terrible offer. We have both of you. You can't get away. You have absolutely no power to negotiate. So how is your 'keep me but let her go' offer going to change our mind? "

"I won't resist," said Charlene.

"Maybe we want you to resist."

Charlene said nothing else.

"Let her go and keep me," said Gertie from her cage. She knew they wouldn't do this, but saying it right after Ken's little speech might add confusion and frustration. Every little bit helped.

"What the hell did I just say?" Ken asked her. "I just finished explaining that you have no negotiating power. Jesus. I guess it's nice that you two aren't trying to sell each other out, but at some point you have to face reality."

"I'm done talking," said Jared. He swung his knife in the air in front of Charlene's face. "I'm ready to start gutting these girls."

"You only get to kill one," said Ken.

"Whatever. I'm ready to get to it."

"Wait, not yet," said Vivian. "I need to get away from the smell for a minute."

"You won't get used to it if you keep going in and out," Ken told her.

"I know, but it's going to make me throw up. Maybe I can find a clothespin or something."

"Just hold your nose."

"I'll be right back," she said, leaving the room. The stairs creaked, and then Gertie heard another door open and close.

"Do we have to wait?" asked Jared.

"Since your mother just asked us to wait, I'm going to say that yes, that's probably what we should do."

Jared ran his index finger over Charlene's chin. "Can I hit her?"

"No."

"Why not?"

"Because it's not what we do."

"It's not what *you* do. I'd like to knock out some of her teeth."

"We're doing this one my way. You catch your own girl, you can punch her all you want."

"Maybe I will."

"And maybe somebody will notice that you've got bruised knuckles. Gosh, that's not suspicious at all when the police sit you down for questioning."

"Whatever."

"How about you ditch the attitude?"

Jared clenched his fist, and for a second Gertie thought he was going to punch Charlene anyway. Instead he slashed his knife across her neck.

CHAPTER SEVENTEEN

"What the hell?" Ken demanded, as blood began to flow.

"I didn't cut her deep."

"Her neck is bleeding. That's deep enough!"

Jared hadn't cut Charlene's throat, but it was a pretty awful slash across the side of her neck. Three thin trickles of blood ran down onto her shirt, joined quickly by a fourth.

Gertie pulled at the bars of the cage, so blinded by rage and terror that she thought the burst of adrenaline might let her bend steel. Of course, it didn't. And there wasn't a damn thing she could do to stop those psychos from hacking up Charlene.

The wound stung and Charlene could feel the blood running down her neck, but with her arms bound she couldn't touch it to see how bad it was. At least she could still breathe.

Ken looked furious. He smacked Jared on the back of

the head so hard that his son dropped the knife. Jared spun around and for an instant Charlene thought the two men might come to blows, but Jared backed away, rubbing his head.

"What was that all about?" Jared asked.

"That is *not* how we do it. You don't just slash out at her like you've gone feral. How long do you think she'll live now?"

"I thought the whole point was to kill her."

"Not like that! If you want to slash somebody's throat, find yourself a prostitute and do it behind a Dumpster. That's not what I'm trying to teach you. Look at all that blood."

"I didn't slash her throat. It's tiny little streams of blood. If we put a Band-Aid on it she'll be fine. I didn't realize you were so concerned about her well-being."

"This was a mistake," said Ken. "Your mom was an idiot for bringing you here."

"Don't call Mom an idiot."

"I didn't call her an idiot. I said she was behaving like an idiot."

"No, you called her an idiot."

"Don't you dare argue with me. I know the circumstances are weird, but I'm still the father and you're still my son. As long as you live in my house and eat the food that I buy, you will respect me. Do you understand?"

Jared seemed to realize that he'd crossed the line. "Yeah, I understand. I've been waiting for this for so long that I got excited. I shouldn't have cut her neck. I'm sorry."

Ken placed his hand on Jared's shoulder. "It's all right. I shouldn't have snapped at you."

Charlene couldn't believe she was witnessing this fucked-up display of father/son reconciliation. They looked like they were going to hug, burst into tears, and tell each other how much they loved them.

"I'm going to check on your mom," said Ken. "I'll only be gone a minute, but you can do anything you want to her. I take that back—nothing sexual. Anything else is okay."

Jared picked the knife up off the floor. "Can I jab out her eyes?"

"If you want. It means she can't see what's going to happen next."

"Seems like that would be scarier."

"No. It's scarier if she can see the knife."

"Maybe I'll only do one eye, then."

"It's totally up to you. Don't touch Gertie."

"I won't."

"Have fun."

"If you wanted to give me an early birthday present, you could leave me here for an hour or so."

"You're lucky you get the minute. Maybe not even that much." Ken walked over to the doorway. "Don't do anything until I'm upstairs. We don't want the neighbors to hear."

Ken left, shutting the door behind him. Charlene assumed this meant there was also an upstairs door blocking the noise from the basement. If she waited for his footsteps to stop creaking, she'd know he'd opened the upstairs door. Yet if she screamed for help, their only option would be to make her stop screaming. That was something she'd save for when she'd accepted that there was no escape and wanted a quick death. For now, she still thought she and Gertie could get out of this.

"I'm a lesbian," she told him.

"So?"

"So I bet you've never been with one, right?"

"No. I'm a dude. That's kind of the whole point of how lesbians work. You must not be very good at it if you don't know that."

"I'm just saying that this opportunity may never happen again. How am I going to stop you?"

"Even if I did want to bang a lesbian—and I do, I'll admit it—I'm not going to do it when my mom could walk into the room at any minute."

"Tell her not to come back down."

Jared's laugh was surprisingly high pitched. "I'm going to pass on trying to rape you with my parents in the house. Like Dad said, you're trying to get me to make a mistake. Not gonna happen. And you don't have to worry about me gouging out your eye. I'm not doing anything to you. Just going to wait patiently for Mom and Dad to come back."

"Pussy."

"Whatever." Jared ran his index and middle fingers across Charlene's neck and licked the blood off of them. "Mmmm," he said with a smile.

"I'm HIV positive," Charlene lied.

Jared let out a horrified gasp and began to frantically wipe at his mouth. He spat onto the floor as he backed away from her.

Gertie kicked him in the back of the head.

There was no sense of accomplishment on her face. Moving her legs had obviously caused her excruciating pain. But she'd done it.

Jared tumbled forward. The knife fell out of his hand and slid across the floor toward Charlene.

Charlene jerked her body to the right. The chair fell onto its side, smashing onto the concrete floor and landing on Jared's hand.

He shrieked.

The arm of the chair hadn't broken on impact, but it had twisted a little. A sharp tug with Charlene's right hand and the arm of the chair popped out of the back. She quickly went to work at getting her hand free. Even if the soundproofing was sufficient to cover Jared's shriek, Ken and Vivian were set to return at any moment.

Jared, now sobbing, pulled his hand free. For right now he was focusing more on his crushed fingers than Charlene's efforts to escape from the ropes.

Charlene got her arm free.

Grabbed for the knife. Missed. Got it on the second try.

Jared might be useful as a hostage, but Charlene was still mostly tied to the chair and she didn't think he'd be focused on his hand long enough for her to completely free herself. So she slammed the knife into his throat.

A gout of warm blood got her in the face.

Jared made horrific gagging noises as he clawed at his neck.

Charlene began to cut away at the rope binding her other hand.

Please let them stay upstairs. Please let them stay upstairs. Please let them stay upstairs.

Jared made an attempt to reach for her, but it was completely ineffectual. Charlene tried not to look at him as she sawed away at the ropes; the grisly sight would distract her.

She cut her left hand free.

Now it would be faster to simply untie the ropes.

Though they hadn't done a careless job of tying her up, they also had obviously planned to be supervising her the whole time she was bound to the chair. She'd be able to untie herself. She just had to pray that they wouldn't come back too soon.

Jared wasn't moving much anymore. The expanding pool of his blood touched Charlene's arm. But if she wasn't worried about her own blood right now, she certainly wasn't going to worry about his. She kept working on the ropes.

"You're doing great," said Gertie.

The ropes were coming apart quickly now.

She heard the stairs creak.

Charlene had already been untying the ropes as fast as she could and there was no way to accelerate the process, even with imminent danger. If she'd had a little more time, she could've lain in wait behind the door. Ken and Vivian would have walked into the room, gaped in horror at their dead son, and she would have killed both of them with the knife. That plan—which wasn't a foolproof one anyway—was off the table now, unless they walked down the stairs very, very slowly.

She got free of the chair just as the doorknob turned.

What to do? Charge across the room at them with the knife?

Minutes ago, Ken still had his gun. She could see the bulge underneath his shirt. There'd be no reason for him to get rid of it. Even if Charlene ran at him faster than she'd ever run in her life, he'd have time to draw the weapon and shoot her in the head.

There was no place to hide.

The door swung open.

Of course, they saw Jared immediately. He was lying

motionless in a large pool of blood and was difficult to miss. In a perfect world, Ken and Vivian would have dropped to their knees, unable to cope with the loss of their offspring. And, in fact, Vivian pushed past her husband and rushed toward the body. But Ken took out his gun.

Charlene jumped up, grabbed hold of the side of Gertie's cage, and pulled herself up. She tried to do this while holding onto the knife, but she dropped it and it clattered onto the floor. She hoped, even in this moment, that her friend would realize that she was not trying to use her as a human shield, but trying to take advantage of Ken's desire to keep Gertie alive. He might not risk accidentally hitting Gertie as he shot at Charlene.

It was entirely possible that Ken no longer gave a shit about Gertie, or at least didn't care in the moments after gazing at his son's bloody corpse, but Charlene had no other option.

Vivian let out a wail of such intense sorrow that Charlene was incapable of not feeling pity for her, even as she could see Ken coming toward the cage, revolver raised.

Charlene pulled herself up higher, so that her head was even with Gertie's. Now she realized that this was absolutely ridiculous. The only way Ken wouldn't be able to kill her was if he laughed so hard at her predicament that he slipped on Jared's blood and knocked himself out. Yes, there was a ninety-nine percent chance that she'd be lying on the floor with her brains scattered around her head if she'd rushed at him, or tried to throw a knife or the chair at him, but at least she would've retained some dignity.

Ken did not seem amused by her predicament. He

walked around to get a good angle at which to shoot her down, so at least she'd been correct—he didn't want to kill Gertie quite yet. Charlene climbed around the cage, trying to keep Gertie between herself and Ken. This tactic would only keep her alive for a few more seconds, but she'd do what she could to make the most of them.

Vivian was on the floor, still wailing as she cradled Jared's body.

Ken kept his distance, as if worried that Charlene had a trick up her sleeve. He was still only a few feet away. It didn't matter that his arm was violently shaking. If he pulled that trigger, he wasn't going to miss.

He pulled the trigger.

Charlene cried out as the bullet tore across her left leg. He hadn't missed, but obviously he'd planned to do much more damage than this. The pain was intense but not enough to make Charlene lose her grip on the cage.

"Don't shoot her!" Vivian screamed, her voice cracking. "Make that fucking bitch suffer!"

Ken set the gun on the ground and stepped forward. Then, apparently deciding he shouldn't leave the gun so close, he kicked it to the other side of the basement.

"Get down from there," said Ken. "Don't make this any worse than it needs to be."

Charlene was pretty sure she'd already maxed out how bad her punishment would be if and when he finally got her down from the cage. She simply braced herself, ready to kick the shit out of him for as long as she could.

"Where do you think you're gonna go?" he asked.

Vivian, no longer wailing, was now whispering to her son. Charlene was glad she couldn't hear the words.

"I asked you a question," said Ken.

Charlene continued to ignore his question, which she'd

assumed was hypothetical. She didn't think she was going anywhere. Even if she had the athletic prowess to leap from cage to cage, it wouldn't do her any good.

Ken moved forward.

Gertie kicked at him. It was a terrible kick, and did little to dissuade him.

"I'll break your goddamn legs," Ken told her.

Gertie kicked at him again, with even less energy.

Charlene had not been dangling from a steel cage all night, so her kick was a lot more vicious. She got him in the chest. But he grabbed her leg and pulled. If it had been the leg that got shot, she suspected that the pain would be so intense that she would have released her grip on the cage and let him do whatever he wanted with her, but instead she yanked her leg free and kicked him in the face.

She didn't hear a satisfying *crack* and he didn't fall to the floor.

He grabbed her injured leg.

The pain was every bit as intense as she'd feared. Yet she didn't let go of the cage. She kicked him with her other leg and her injured leg popped out of his hands.

She glanced down at him. Ken looked absolutely batshit insane with rage.

He let out a furious bellow that was even louder and more unhinged than Vivian's wailing.

Charlene climbed as high as she could. There wasn't room for her to perch on top of the cage, but she was right up against the ceiling.

Ken picked up the knife that had been used to kill his son. "*You can't get away from me!*" he screamed.

He grabbed the bars and pulled himself up. The cage suddenly tilted toward him.

And then the cage, which probably had not been installed with the intention of supporting the weight of three people, came free of the ceiling.

For a heartbeat, it seemed to float in midair. It felt like that moment right before a rollercoaster goes down the first terrifying hill.

Then the cage crashed down onto the floor.

It landed on its side, crushing Ken beneath it.

The cage rolled over, but his ruined body was stuck to it and went along for the short ride.

Charlene had injured something in the impact, maybe even broken a bone, but she'd worry about that later. She leapt off the cage, toward the corner where Ken had kicked the revolver.

Vivian's sense of self-preservation clearly outweighed her need to be with her dead family. She hurried out of the room and slammed the door shut behind her. There was a beep on the other side.

Charlene picked up the gun and staggered back to the cage. She hadn't even thought about whether she'd be able to walk on her injured leg—she'd just done it. It was a little difficult to breathe, but not painful, so she suspected that she had bruised ribs rather than broken ones.

Her first task was to see if Ken was still a threat.

He was not. His body was no longer stuck to the cage, and he wasn't dead yet, but at least three different bones were visible and he was choking on his own blood. She wasn't going to waste a bullet putting him out of his misery.

She turned her attention to Gertie, who lay unmoving in the cage.

Blood had soaked through Gertie's pants on her upper

thighs. If the cage had fallen straight down it would have shattered Gertie's legs, but despite the blood her injuries didn't seem horrific. No limbs appeared to be twisted. And as she watched carefully, she could see that Gertie was breathing. Though Charlene wasn't prepared to give her a clean bill of health quite yet, she was pretty sure that Gertie had just been knocked unconscious in the fall.

She went over to the door and tested the knob. Locked. There was a keypad next to the door, so she went back to Ken and crouched next to him.

"What's the code?" she asked.

He opened his mouth—barely—but no sound came out.

"Tell me the code or I'll break your fingers."

Though his mouth moved, she was pretty sure that even if she'd been able to hear what he was saying, it would not have been the combination.

Then his mouth stopped moving and his whole body went still.

Okay. They were locked in the basement. But Charlene had a gun. As soon as Vivian opened the door to check on them, she'd shoot her. No problem.

This assumed that Vivian *did* check on them.

If the basement was soundproofed, and her husband and son were dead, she might have no motive to check on them. At least not anytime soon.

Charlene suddenly became very much aware of how much blood had spilled from her neck onto her clothes.

CHAPTER EIGHTEEN

Charlene began to feel dizzy. With the immediate danger over and the adrenaline no longer rocketing through her veins, the severity of her injuries was becoming clear.

She shook it off. She still had shit to do. Maybe Vivian was going to leave them down here to die, but if she didn't, Charlene had to be ready.

Moving as quickly as she could with a body that was no longer fully cooperating, Charlene picked up the knife and cut away a non-bloody part of the leg of Ken's pants. She tied it around her neck, tight enough to hopefully hold off the bleeding without choking her. She cut off another strip of his pants and tied it around her leg, much tighter than around her neck.

It wasn't much. It might not get her through the night. But since she hadn't been locked down here with a first aid kit, it would have to do.

She checked the cage door. It was held shut with a padlock. She could possibly shoot it off with the revolver, but she'd be squandering a bullet she might need later. Gertie wouldn't be able to walk, much less help her fight Vivian, so there was no reason to try to free her from the cage yet. Though she would try to wake her up.

Ken had taken the smelling salts with him when he left earlier. Charlene reached through the bars and patted her leg. "Gertie? Hey, Gertie?"

Gertie, though still breathing, did not stir.

What if she'd bashed her head hard enough to cause brain damage?

That wasn't something to worry about right now. Until she discovered otherwise, she'd assume that Gertie was unconscious but perfectly fine.

Maybe it was for the better that she wasn't waking up. As long as she was asleep, she didn't know that she was in a cage within a cage.

Charlene felt that she was doing a surprisingly good job of staying calm, considering that she was bleeding from the neck and leg and surrounded by carnage. Not too long ago she'd been haunted by memories of Lee killing himself, which she'd assumed would be the most horrific sight of her lifetime. She'd never expected to surpass it so soon. Jared's pool of blood was still slowly expanding, and Ken's body was just a mangled mess.

She walked back to the door. She wasn't sure which side was best for an ambush. On the left, she could shoot as soon as it opened a crack. On the right, the door would hide her until Vivian stepped inside. But either way, Vivian knew she had a loaded gun, and she'd take precautions.

If she ever opened the door.

Let them rot down there. Let those bitches rot.

Vivian opened some kitchen cabinets and quickly found a bottle of whiskey. She unscrewed the cap and downed a large gulp. Then she had a huge coughing fit, stumbled over to the sink, and vomited.

She'd lost everything.

Her son and husband were dead. She'd never see them again, because she was never going back down into that basement. Both doors were locked. Charlene would probably bleed out before she starved, but she hoped Gertie died a slow, lingering, agonizing death.

Vivian didn't believe in ghosts. But maybe the ghosts of Jared and Ken would stay in that room, tormenting the girls until they finally succumbed to their demise. Perhaps continuing to torment them in hell.

She took another drink of whiskey, this time without vomiting.

She'd clean herself up, then find a place to dispose of the bodies in the trunk of her car. Then she'd go home and do nothing. Eventually she'd call the police and report her family missing, but since they'd gone on a weeklong father/son camping trip with unreliable cell phone service, she hadn't been worried. She'd have plenty of time to practice her response when the police informed her of what her husband and son had really been doing.

She went into the bathroom and turned on the faucet, making sure not to look in the mirror. If she saw her reflection now, it was the only way she'd ever see herself.

The doorbell rang.

Fuck.

Vivian couldn't ignore it. There'd been a lot of chaos

in the basement, and not all of the sound had been masked. If she didn't convince whoever was at the door that everything was fine, they'd surely call the cops. Assuming it wasn't the cops at her door.

Her clothes were drenched in blood. She could strip out of them, but she'd still have blood all over her, and there was no time to rinse off. Instead, she hurried to the door.

"May I help you?" she asked.

"Hi," said a man on the other side. "We're your neighbors. We wanted to make sure everything was okay."

"It's fine. Everything here is totally fine." Did she sound hysterical? Vivian thought she might sound hysterical. That was not the tone she wanted to convey. "Sorry I can't open the door, I was in the shower when I heard the doorbell and I'm not decent."

"No problem, no problem," said the man. "We heard some commotion over here. Sounded like screaming."

"Yes, that was the TV. I was watching a horror movie too loud. I'm sorry—I didn't realize the sound carried that far."

"Sounds like a crazy flick. Which movie? We'll have to check it out."

"I don't remember the title. They're all pretty much the same, right?"

"Are you sure everything's okay?" a woman asked.

"It's all good. I apologize for not coming over to introduce myself sooner. I don't actually live here."

"No, no, that's fine," said the man. "We're sorry for bothering you. Maybe we can get together for coffee sometime."

"Yes, absolutely. That would be great. Again, I

apologize for not opening the door—I'm standing here dripping all over."

"Then we'll let you dry off. We're glad everything is okay. Talk to you later."

"Yes, talk to you later," said Vivian. She wanted to open the curtain to peek at them, but she didn't want them to see her peeking.

The only way that could've gone worse was if they were actually the cops and they kicked down the door. She'd babbled her way through that conversation and she knew with one hundred percent certainty that they were going to call the police as soon as they got back home, if they weren't dialing 911 already.

She'd have to kill them.

No. That was stupid and psychotic. She couldn't believe her mind had gone there. She couldn't just chase after them and stab them to death right in the front yard. What if there were other people at their house? What if they had kids? What if they successfully fended her off? Committing a long string of murders was not the way out of this.

She could still claim innocence. Could still pretend to be the oblivious wife who was completely unaware of the sinister activities of her husband and son.

Only two people could contradict her story.

She couldn't wait them out. She didn't know how difficult it would be for the authorities to get past the two electronic locks, but she assumed that they could do it before Charlene and Gertie died.

Vivian had to get rid of them as quickly as possible.

Charlene tensed up as she heard a beep on the other side of the door, followed by a click that she assumed was the lock disengaging.

The door didn't open.

She waited.

She wasn't sure if she'd shoot at the first sign of movement on the other side, or if she'd wait to be sure it was Vivian. She didn't want to survive this nightmare only to accidentally murder a police officer who was there to rescue her.

Charlene continued to wait. Was Vivian out there working up the courage to come inside? Was it a trap?

Of course it was a trap. Vivian wasn't going to simply set her free. This was absolutely without question a trap. But Charlene had to go out there, even with a trap about to spring, because her other choice was to bleed to death in the basement.

She very slowly turned the doorknob. Then she shoved the door open as hard as she could, hoping that if Vivian was standing outside it would bash into her.

The door didn't bash into anything.

Charlene listened carefully for the sound of breathing, though it would be hard to hear over her own gasps for air.

The only light came from the cage room. Charlene could see up the stairs, which were empty, but not much to her left or right. There was a light switch right next to the door, but when Charlene flipped it on and off nothing happened.

She slowly crept up the stairs. It couldn't be this easy. Either the door would be locked, or Vivian would be waiting on the other side, seated in a chair with a double barrel shotgun in her lap.

The stairs creaked with each step, which terrified her, even though Vivian almost certainly knew where she was without the sound.

At the top of the stairs, Charlene turned the knob. The door was locked.

She looked at the keypad. She had no idea what Ken might use for his four-digit code. She might as well try *something*, and it had letters underneath each number like on a phone, so she punched in 2-2-4-3.

C-A-G-E.

The display reset and the door did not unlock.

"Vivian" and "Jared" both had more than four letters. And though Charlene wasn't sure how these kinds of locks worked, a computer would lock you out if you got the password wrong too many times, so she didn't want to keep trying and risk a scenario where even Vivian couldn't get them out of the basement.

She again considered the idea of shooting the lock.

But, again, she didn't know what would happen. Obviously, if she blew apart the keypad the lock wouldn't conveniently slide open. If she tried to shoot the lock itself, she might make it worse, jam it to the point where it couldn't open. If she had a double-barrel shotgun, yeah, she'd blow the shit out of it, but with a revolver it seemed like a dumb thing to do.

So she crept back down the stairs.

Vivian didn't have a gun. That seemed obvious. Otherwise, she would've shot Charlene by now. That was a small consolation as she glanced around the dark area, trying to figure out where Vivian might be hiding if she was actually down here, but at least it was a consolation.

It occurred to her that she hadn't tried to negotiate. It

probably wouldn't work this time, either, yet it was still worth trying.

"Hey!" she called out. "Are you down here?"

Vivian didn't answer.

"You didn't do anything," said Charlene. "We'll tell that to the police. We'll tell it to everybody. You tried to stop them. We can end this without you getting shot."

No response.

Charlene wanted to sit down. All of that talking was exhausting.

Damn. She really *was* going to bleed to death.

Without the ticking clock of bleeding out, she could just perch herself upon the top step and wait for Vivian to eventually reveal herself. But now she didn't think she had a choice but to go on the offensive.

Left or right?

She didn't know where either direction led, so it didn't matter. She walked to the left. After a couple of steps, some shards of glass crunched underneath her shoe. Probably a light bulb. If Vivian had bothered to knock out the light bulbs, she most likely was indeed hiding down here.

Charlene walked slowly, gun extended, finger on the trigger.

Her eyes had adjusted to the darkness enough that she could see that she was in a laundry room. Nothing out of the ordinary: a washer, dryer, and a couple of empty baskets. No apparent place for Vivian to hide, unless she'd climbed into the dryer, which was unlikely.

Movement behind her.

She spun around. The door to the cage room was all the way open. Then it closed.

Shit!

Charlene rushed over there. She momentarily lost her balance but didn't fall. She reached for the doorknob—

—just as the door flew back open, smashing into Charlene and knocking her off her feet. She landed on her back, hard, and a few drops of blood shot into the air.

It took a second for her vision to focus. When it did, Vivian hovered over her, swinging something down at her with both hands.

Upon impact, intense pain shot through Charlene's arm and then her hand went numb. Vivian struck her twice more. It was a riding crop, something you'd use on a horse or a kinky sex partner. Charlene tried to twist her hand around, so she could pull the trigger and put a bullet in Vivian's face, but her hand wasn't cooperating.

She couldn't lose the gun. She could survive repeated hits with a riding crop, but if Vivian got the revolver, Charlene was dead. And then Gertie right after that.

Vivian continued to strike Charlene's arm, which now had several bloody streaks on it.

If Charlene wasn't weak from blood loss, she'd be kicking Vivian's ass for sure. As it stood, she couldn't really do much but lie there and take her punishment.

Vivian switched her target, smacking the riding crop across Charlene's face. It hurt so badly that she didn't immediately register that Vivian had yanked the gun out of her hand.

Charlene curled the fingers of her other hand into a claw and swung at Vivian's face. Long fingernails were not conducive to waitressing or lesbian activities, so she kept hers clipped short, which was inconvenient right now. But she got Vivian in the mouth just as the woman was screaming at her, getting her index and middle fingers between Vivian's teeth and cheek. She yanked hard, hoping to tear off part of Vivian's face.

Her cheek did not rip wide open, but blood appeared at the corner of her mouth as Charlene's fingers popped free.

Then Charlene punched her in the brand new wound.

Vivian howled in pain.

She still held the gun, and Charlene saw that the gun was pointed right at her chest. As soon as Vivian gained the presence of mind to squeeze the trigger, there was going to be a great big hole very close to her heart.

Charlene punched her again. Vivian, who was actually foaming at the mouth as if she'd gone rabid, tried to bite her fist. Her teeth scraped against the back of Charlene's hand, tearing away skin, but didn't sink in deep.

Vivian let out a cry that sounded more animal than human. The woman had completely, utterly lost her mind. But she still had the gun.

Summoning all of her strength, Charlene rolled over, just as Vivian fired. The bullet pounded into the floor. Charlene sat up, which hurt like hell, and grabbed Vivian's wrist. She pulled it backwards, trying to snap the bones, and when that didn't work she tried to dig what existed of her fingernails into Vivian's flesh.

Vivian twisted the gun around and squeezed off another shot. This one flew past Charlene's shoulder. Her ears were now ringing so badly that she could barely hear Vivian's primal shriek.

Charlene still held Vivian's wrist. She squeezed tighter and tighter, hoping her fingers would burst right through Vivian's skin. Finally, the gun slipped out of Vivian's fingers and landed on Charlene's leg.

She immediately grabbed the weapon. Vivian lunged

for it as well. There was no time to get her finger around the trigger, take aim, and fire, so Charlene settled for flinging the gun away from them, toward the laundry room.

Vivian, perhaps taking a cue from Charlene punching the wound on her face, smacked the gash on Charlene's neck. Charlene couldn't really hear the sound her own voice made, but she assumed that it too was less than human.

Charlene tried to make another plea for them to just go their separate ways, but her mouth wasn't successfully forming words anymore. She punched at Vivian but missed completely. Vivian spat some blood into Charlene's face, then got up and staggered toward the laundry room.

Though her body felt like it was going to split apart and just start spraying blood from a dozen places, Charlene forced herself to stand up and go after her. She hadn't lost yet.

But when Vivian picked up the gun, Charlene was still ten feet away. No way to tackle her before she could shoot. Instead, Charlene began to back away, hoping she wouldn't slip on her own blood.

"Please..." she said, or thought she said, even though there was absolutely no chance of reasoning with the woman at this point.

Vivian pointed the gun at her. When she smiled—a crazed, scary smile—blood streamed from both sides of her mouth.

There was a knock at the door at the top of the stairs.

Somebody was inside the house.

Vivian looked up at it. If Charlene had been closer to her, this would have been a perfect distraction, an opportunity to attack and try to wrestle the gun out of her hand. Hell, if she'd had anything that she could throw, the knock at the door might have saved her life. Instead, all it did was buy her enough time to take a couple more steps back.

The knocking continued. More of a pounding now.

Vivian didn't lower the gun. She squeezed the trigger.

Missed, though not by much. Charlene took another step back.

Vivian fired again. This shot took a piece out of Charlene's shoulder. A few inches to the left and it would have struck the same place that Jared slashed her neck.

She hadn't won yet. Charlene wasn't going to give up until she was dead.

Vivian took a few steps forward, to get better aim.

"*Please...*" Charlene repeated.

The pounding continued.

Charlene cried out and doubled over as Vivian shot her in the stomach.

She fell to the floor, gasping for breath. Blood was already pooling beneath her.

Vivian wiped the blood off her mouth, then turned away from Charlene and walked into the room with the cages.

Charlene wanted to shout out a warning to Gertie, as worthless as that would be, but right now, and possibly forever, there wasn't a damn thing she could do.

CHAPTER NINETEEN

Vivian almost wanted to sob with relief as she turned away from that bitch. If she was quick, she could kill Gertie, then finish off Charlene if she wasn't dead already. She'd have to figure out a narrative that made sense, but if she acted hysterical— that is, if she continued to act hysterical—nobody would expect her to share her story right away. She could go mute until she'd worked things out.

She almost dropped to her knees as she saw the gory corpses of Jared and Ken, but forced herself to look past that. She just needed to kill Gertie, a helpless unconscious girl in a cage, and everything would be all right.

She took the long way around to avoid stepping in any blood.

Gertie, obviously, hadn't gone anywhere.

Vivian walked up to the cage. Gertie's eyes were closed but she was still breathing. Vivian didn't get too close, in case it was a trick, but she pointed the barrel of the revolver at Gertie's forehead and squeezed the trigger.

Nothing happened. Just a click.

Was she out of bullets? She'd only fired five times.

Wait, she'd forgotten about Ken shooting Charlene in the leg. Yes, the gun was out of bullets. She tossed it onto the floor. Her fingerprints were all over the weapon, but she'd probably have to admit to shooting Charlene anyway, since their blood was mixed together out there. She'd just claim self-defense.

Gertie's death would obviously not be self-defense. She'd blame this one on Ken.

She looked around for the knife. It was lying on the floor. The pool of Jared's blood had reached it, but she'd have to get over her revulsion and pick it up. No time to hesitate. She let out an anguished sob as she picked up the dripping weapon.

Vivian returned to the cage and reached inside with the knife. Three or four quick stabs in the center of the throat and Gertie would no longer be able to tell the truth about what happened.

Gertie's eyes flew open and she grabbed Vivian's arm.

Gertie had awakened to the sounds of screams. She didn't waste energy trying to get out of the cage, but she did flex her arms, trying to get the blood circulating. The pins and needles sensation was pure agony.

She'd popped at least one set of stitches in her leg when she kicked the kid, and possibly the other when the cage fell, so the legs of her pants were soaked with blood.

She'd listened to the sounds of Charlene and Vivian's fight, wishing she were out there to help break Vivian's arms and legs.

She'd heard what sounded like pounding. Was somebody trying to get into the basement?

Heard the gunshots.

When the door swung open, she'd prayed that it would be Charlene, there to rescue her. Upon seeing that it was Vivian, she'd immediately closed her eyes.

She forced herself to keep them closed as Vivian walked over to the cage.

Somehow, she didn't flinch at the sound of a click. Had Vivian tried to shoot her?

When she could tell that Vivian's arm was inside the cage, she moved.

Grabbed Vivian's arm.

Pulled it down.

It didn't hurt Vivian, but her long blonde hair spilled down into the cage.

Gertie grabbed Vivian's hair with her other hand. Twisted it around her fist. All of Gertie's fingers were raw and sore from the knife-under-the-fingernails treatment, but she gritted her teeth and fought through the excruciating pain.

Yanked as hard as she could.

Vivian's face bashed into the cage, chin-first. She dropped the knife.

Gertie yanked again.

Vivian smashed into the steel again. Her nose split open.

Vivian screamed something incoherent and tried to pull her head away, but Gertie was able to pull her hair one more time, bashing her right on the mouth. As Vivian screamed, a couple of her front teeth dropped into the cage.

The woman's face was a ghastly sight but she was still

very much alive.

Gertie had no strength left to yank her hair again.

She did have enough strength—barely—to pick up the knife and jab it up through the bars.

Gertie was aiming for her neck, right where Charlene had stabbed Jared. But Vivian had moved. The blade plunged into her heart instead.

As blood pumped down upon Gertie, Vivian tried to push herself back up to a standing position. A moment later, she dropped to the floor. It would've been a sick, fucked-up romantic ending if she'd landed on top of her husband, but Ken's corpse was on the other side of the cage.

Gertie wiped Vivian's blood out of her eyes. Some had gotten directly on her right eyeball and she frantically tried to blink it out to make the burning sensation disappear.

It wasn't going away. She'd worry about that later.

She called out to Charlene, who didn't answer.

She kept calling out, even though she'd heard multiple gunshots, and the fact that Charlene was not in the room with her right now was a pretty strong indication that her friend was dead.

There was a loud crash outside of the room.

Creaking on the stairs. Too much creaking to be only one person.

"We've got a body!" a man shouted.

Two men walked into the cage room. Police officers. If she'd been able to give them some sort of warning about what they'd see, she would have. She would have warned them about the now-eleven cages dangling from the ceiling, most of them with dead bodies inside. Warned them about the teenage boy lying with an open throat in a pool of blood. Warned them about the dead man who'd been crushed by a heavy steel cage. Warned them about the woman with blood gushing from her heart.

The cops looked like they could have used the warning. One of them immediately turned around and vomited, while the other gaped at the nightmares surrounding him.

The one who'd vomited removed his walkie-talkie from his belt and stepped back out of the room. She heard him say something frantic about needing backup and an ambulance, immediately.

Immediately.

You didn't need an ambulance immediately to collect dead people.

Of course, it could've been meant for her, but Gertie wasn't sure the cop had even noticed that she was still alive before he left the room.

She tried to wave for the other cop's attention, but her arms had moved all they were going to for now. "I'm alive," she managed to say.

The cop hurried over to the cage, eyes wide. He tugged on the door but it didn't open.

"We'll get you out of there," he promised her.

"How's my friend?" she asked.

The cop glanced at the three corpses, as if uncertain about what kind of news he'd have to deliver. "Which one's your friend?"

"She's outside."

"I'm not sure. My partner is checking her out. Worry about yourself for now."

"I don't need to. I'm fine."

Gertie was pretty sure her stab wounds were getting

infected, and she didn't know yet what injuries she'd sustained when the cage fell, and she was certain she'd have nightmares every night for approximately the next seventy years, but as long as Charlene wasn't right outside the door with her brains splashed against the wall, Gertie believed that things would indeed be fine.

It felt like it took forever for a police officer to show up with bolt cutters. By then, Charlene had already been taken away in an ambulance. She wasn't dead yet. The cop who'd told her to worry about herself gravely informed Gertie that Charlene had a nasty neck wound and had been shot in the leg, which Gertie already knew, and that she'd been shot directly in the stomach.

She was unconscious and unresponsive. But alive.

"She's got a rough time ahead," the cop said. "But if she can stick it out until they get her into surgery, I think she'll pull through."

Charlene Fox stuck it out until they got her into surgery.

EPILOGUE

Charlene and Gertie sat across from each other in the restaurant booth, sipping their non-alcoholic chocolate milkshakes.

They'd spent a lot of time together, with Gertie visiting her every single day during her stay in Intensive Care, then every single day after she got moved to a regular room, and then every single day after she moved to inpatient physical therapy. Gertie was who she saw when she opened her eyes for the first time after that bitch shot her in the gut, though Gertie had immediately rushed off to the waiting room to let Charlene's parents know she was finally awake.

She'd thought she might resent having Gertie around so much, as a reminder that she'd been responsible for dragging her into this nightmare in the first place, but she actually found Gertie's presence very comforting. And they'd continued to see each other on that wonderful day when inpatient therapy became outpatient therapy.

Best friends forever? Sure, why not?

Gertie didn't know if this counted as a victory or not.

She had not saved her cousin Kimberly. Had not saved Ken's latest victim. Had definitely been responsible for Travis getting on Vivian's radar, and was thus also responsible for the other two victims that showed up at the wrong time.

Three innocent deaths because of her involvement.

How many more women would Ken have kidnapped if he'd been allowed to continue?

More than three?

She'd never know.

Maybe Jared would have followed in his father's footsteps.

Gertie may have saved a large number of hypothetical victims. And she may have saved none. She'd just have to satisfy herself with the knowledge that the bad people were dead.

"This is a good shake," said Charlene.

"I know."

"It would be better with some rum in it."

"You can't have alcohol."

"I'm just saying. You could have some rum in yours, and let me smell it."

"I'm not going to drink a delicious alcoholic milkshake in front of you."

"That's very kind of you. You're a good friend. When are you going to go down on me?"

"I'm not."

"I think you owe that to me. You have to eat my pussy for all you put me through."

"In your dreams."

"They're actually nightmares. You'd be terrible at it. You'd be all like—" Charlene stuck out her tongue in random directions to mimic poor oral sex technique. "It would be embarrassing. I'd eventually just get bored and leave."

"People are staring at you."

"I got my neck slashed open by one psychopath, I got shot in the stomach by another psychopath, and I was almost locked in a cage to starve to death by a third psychopath. Guess how much I care that people are staring at my tongue?"

"I got stabbed a few times by a psychopath, and I *did* get locked in a cage to starve to death, and I do care that people are staring at your tongue."

"Too bad for you. I'm sure they're silently judging you. Can you feel their eyes boring into the back of your head?"

Gertie laughed. "I'm glad you're back to normal."

"Oh, I'm so far from normal that it isn't even funny."

"You're back to acting like you did when I first met you."

Charlene picked up her milkshake glass. "We should do a toast."

"To what?"

"I don't know. To anything. To not getting murdered by a family of serial killers."

Gertie held up her glass. "To not getting murdered by a family of serial killers."

They clinked their glasses together and drank their chocolate milkshakes.

- The End -

ACKNOWLEDGMENTS

Thanks to my usual amazing crew of Tod Clark, Donna Fitzpatrick, Lynne Hansen, Michael McBride, Jim Morey, Paul Synuria II, and Rhonda Rettig for their assistance with this novel. Thanks also to the ghosts of Roan Mountain, Tennessee, for letting me finish this book in peace when they could've been jerks and possessed the other people in the cabin.

OTHER BOOKS BY JEFF STRAND

Remember: Readers who leave reviews deserve great big hugs!

Ferocious. The creatures of the forest are dead...and hungry!

Bring Her Back. A tale of revenge and madness.

Sick House. A home invasion from beyond the grave.

Bang Up. A filthy comedic thriller. "You want to pay me to sleep with your wife?" is just the start of the story.

Cold Dead Hands. Ten people are trapped in a freezer during a terrorist attack on a grocery store.

How You Ruined My Life (Young Adult). Sixteen-year-old Rod has a pretty cool life until his cousin Blake moves in and slowly destroys everything he holds dear.

Everything Has Teeth. A third collection of short tales of horror and macabre comedy.

An Apocalypse of Our Own. Can the Friend Zone survive the end of the world?

Stranger Things Have Happened (Young Adult). Teenager Marcus Millian III is determined to be one of the greatest magicians who ever lived. Can he make a live shark disappear from a tank?

Cyclops Road. When newly widowed Evan Portin gives a woman named Harriett a ride out of town, she says she's on a cross-country journey to slay a Cyclops. Is she crazy, or...?

Blister. While on vacation, cartoonist Jason Tray meets the town legend, a hideously disfigured woman who lives in a shed.

The Greatest Zombie Movie Ever (Young Adult). Three best friends with more passion than talent try to make the ultimate zombie epic.

Kumquat. A road trip comedy about TV, hot dogs, death, and obscure fruit.

I Have a Bad Feeling About This (Young Adult). Geeky, non-athletic Henry Lambert is sent to survival camp, which is bad enough *before* the trio of murderous thugs show up.

Pressure. What if your best friend was a killer...and he wanted you to be just like him? Bram Stoker Award nominee for Best Novel.

Dweller. The lifetime story of a boy and his monster. Bram Stoker Award nominee for Best Novel.

A Bad Day For Voodoo. A young adult horror/comedy about why sticking pins in a voodoo doll of your history teacher isn't always the best idea. Bram Stoker Award nominee for Best Young Adult Novel.

Dead Clown Barbecue. A collection of demented stories about severed noses, ventriloquist dummies, giant-sized vampires, sibling stabbings, and lots of other messed-up stuff.

Dead Clown Barbecue Expansion Pack. A few more stories for those who couldn't get enough.

Wolf Hunt. Two thugs for hire. One beautiful woman. And one vicious frickin' werewolf.

Wolf Hunt 2. New wolf. Same George and Lou.

The Sinister Mr. Corpse. The feel-good zombie novel of the year.

Benjamin's Parasite. A rather disgusting action/horror/comedy about why getting infected with a ghastly parasite is unpleasant.

Fangboy. A dark and demented fairy tale for adults.

Kutter. A serial killer finds a Boston terrier, and it might just make him into a better person.

Faint of Heart. To get her kidnapped husband back, Melody has to relive her husband's nightmarish weekend, step-by-step...and survive.

Mandibles. Giant killer ants wreaking havoc in the big city!

Stalking You Now. A twisty-turny thriller soon to be the feature film *Mindy Has To Die.*

Graverobbers Wanted (No Experience Necessary). First in the Andrew Mayhem series.

Single White Psychopath Seeks Same. Second in the Andrew Mayhem series.

Casket For Sale (Only Used Once). Third in the Andrew Mayhem series.

Lost Homicidal Maniac (Answers to "Shirley"). Fourth in the Andrew Mayhem series.

The Andrew Mayhem Collection. All four novels for one low price!

Suckers (with JA Konrath). Andrew Mayhem meets Harry McGlade. Which one will prove to be more incompetent?

Gleefully Macabre Tales. A collection of thirty-two demented tales. Bram Stoker Award nominee for Best Collection.

Elrod McBugle on the Loose. A comedy for kids (and adults who were warped as kids).

The Haunted Forest Tour (with Jim Moore). The greatest theme park attraction in the world! Take a completely safe ride through an actual haunted forest! Just hope that your tram doesn't break down, because this forest is PACKED with monsters...

Draculas (with JA Konrath, Blake Crouch, and F. Paul Wilson). An outbreak of feral vampires in a secluded hospital. This one isn't much like *Twilight.*

For information on all of these books, visit Jeff Strand's more-or-less official website at http://www.jeffstrand.com

Subscribe to Jeff Strand's free monthly newsletter (which includes a brand new story in every issue) at http://eepurl.com/bpv5br

Printed in Great Britain
by Amazon